Reclaiming Medusa

Reclaiming Medusa

Short Stories by Contemporary Puerto Rican Women

Edited and Translated by Diana Vélez

spinsters / *aunt lute*

SAN FRANCISCO

Copyright © 1988 Diana Vélez

First Edition
10-9-8-7-6-5-4-3-2-1

Spinsters/Aunt Lute Book Company
P.O. Box 410687
San Francisco, CA 94141

Spinsters/Aunt Lute is an educational project of the Capp Street Founda-
tion. The publication of this book is made possible, in part, with public
funds from the National Endowment for the Arts.

Cover and Text Design: Pam Wilson Design Studio
Cover Art: Pam Wilson
Typesetting: Comp-Type, Fort Bragg, CA
Production: Martha Davis   Rosana Francescato
                Suzanne Israel   Terry Newson
                Debra DeBondt   Lorraine Grassano
                Cindy Lamb   Kathleen Wilkinson

Printed in the U.S.A.

Library of Congress Cataloging-in-Publication Data
Vélez, Diana L.
    Reclaiming Medusa.

    1. Short stories, Puerto Rican—Translations into English. 2. Short
stories, English—Translations from Spanish. 3. Puerto Rican fiction—
Women authors. 4. Puerto Rican fiction—20th century. I. Vélez, Diana L.
PQ7436.S5R4   1988   863'.01'089287—dc19   88-11430

ISBN: 0-933216-41-6

"The Youngest Doll" originally appeared in *Feminist Studies* Vol. 12, #2, Summer
1986. "La bella durmiente" originally appeared in *Papeles de Pandora* México, D.F.:
Joaquín Mortiz, 1979. "Pico Rico Mandorico" originally appeared in *La mona que le
pisaron la cola* San Juan: Instituto de Cultura Puertorriqueña. "Milagros, Calle
Mercurio" and "Pilar, tus rizos" originally appeared in *Vírgenes y mártires* Rio
Piedras, P.R.: Editorial Antillana, 1981. "Veintitres y una tortuga" and "Anoche por la
mañana" originally appeared in *Veintitres y una tortuga* San Juan: Instituto de
Cultura Puertorriqueña, 1981. "Diario 1" and "Diario 6" originally appeared in
Diarios Robados Buenos Aires: Ediciones de la Flor, 1982. "Tres aerobicos para el
amor" and "Ajustes, S.A." originally appeared in *Pasión de historia . . . y otras
historias de pasión* Buenos Aires: Ediciones de la Flor, 1987.

Acknowledgements

━━━━━━━━━━━━━━━━━━━

" . . . give her a room of her own
and five hundred a year . . . ."
— *Virginia Woolf*

I would like to thank the University of Iowa for granting me a developmental assignment which allowed me time to prepare the bulk of the manuscript for this book. Thanks are also due the University of Iowa's University House for its generous assistance, and to Joan Pinkvoss for her sensitive, intelligent editing.

Table of Contents

Introduction 1
Translator's Preface 19

Rosario Ferré
The Youngest Doll 27
Sleeping Beauty 34
Pico Rico, Mandorico 64
Pico Rico, Mandorico (Spanish original) 73

Carmen Lugo Filippi
Milagros, on Mercurio Street 87
Pilar, Your Curls 101

Mayra Montero
Thirteen and a Turtle 111
Veintitres y una tortuga (Spanish original) 117
Last Night at Dawn 123

Carmen Valle
Diary Entry #6 133
Diary Entry #1 135

Ana Lydia Vega
Three Love Aerobics 143
ADJ, Inc. 149

Reclaiming
Medusa

Introduction

"For there is always this to be said for the literary profession—like life itself, it provides its own revenges and antidotes."
—Elizabeth Janeway[1]

"The kernel of the myth is, that there existed somewhere a creature of aspect so terrible that those who saw her turned at once into stone."
—H. J. Rose,
A Handbook of Greek Mythology[2]

What power! And who can keep from envying it, despite its fearful consequences? For although one late version of the myth gives us a beautiful Medusa—"coldly and calmly beautiful" according to H. J. Rose—the more common version is the ugly monster whose severed head, a mass of writhing serpents, hangs from the hand of Perseus.[3] Clearly, Medusa has not had good press. But what if we were to ask, as Teresa de Lauretis does in her insightful essay on narrative, what did Medusa feel as she gazed into Perseus' shield?[4] And why, indeed, is the question never asked? Why are we always pushed, as readers, into an identification with Perseus, the hero who appropriated Medusa's power? But, as no myth consists of only one version, and since feminism is, among other things, a reclaiming of lost power, perhaps we can ask, by re-membering Medusa, what stories each of her strands would tell. For though she could not be gazed at, she herself could see. And what would be Medusa's desire? Probably revenge. And what better way to get it than through writing. Writing, which provides its own revenges and antidotes.

THE POETICS OF TEXTUAL REVENGE

It would be inaccurate to speak of all the stories collected here as revenge narratives, but it does seem that each one unmasks patriarchy—lays it bare—in a way that avenges at least some of the wrongs done to women in its name. Each story also has a peculiar, unexpected twist at the end, a surprise or a contradiction which opens up a space for various readings. Among these readings, quite often, is one of revenge. For even when the story ends merely in a contradiction or a question, the text provides the reader with enough material to construct for herself a pleasure-giving ending wherein the heroine "gets even." Or, failing that, the writing process may itself be a vengeful act, as when the author depicts the ups and downs of being female in contemporary Puerto Rico in such a way—say through irony or humor—that "masculinity" is stripped of its pretensions—a keen, though non-violent, form of revenge. Writing is a complex working out of wishes, and since daydreaming and artistic production both stem from the same source, all art may be best described as serious play.[5] Thus, as the writer inscribes her desire through the symbolic order of language, she weaves narratives which, in their imaginative relation to her life, undercut its suffocating reality. By creating fictional worlds, the author is engaged in a utopian venture which, in the case of the stories collected here, is feminist in nature.

For if there is a commonality of spirit in these stories, it lies in their creation of a space in which the socially pre-scribed "woman's place" is questioned, problematized, and often, subverted. This questioning is culturally specific: we're looking at contemporary Puerto Rico, post-Operation Boot-strap Puerto Rico, industrialized though still colonized, com-plete with Burger Kings and Kentucky Fried Chickens. And "a woman's place" as defined by the patriarchal order there, despite its strong resemblance to its mainland counterpart, fits into its own set of codes—cultural, linguistic, literary. These define "woman" in a peculiarly Puerto Rican way.

There are violations of many codes in these texts, numerous subversions of power. Just in terms of the linguistic code, for example, the active—even aggressive—voices of "Three Love Aerobics" violate norms which define proper language for women. Their language should be gentle, non-threatening, even nurturing. Moreover, women—and by extension, female narrators—should not refer to sexual things by their names. Euphemisms should be used. Certainly the second of these aerobics violates this norm because of its sexual combativeness. Various cultural and religious codes in Puerto Rico classify all women as either "good" women or whores, and one of the criteria for making this judgment is the way in which a woman speaks. So Ana Lydia Vega's use and creative transformation of common street language—its var-ious dialects, jargons and styles—is a direct challenge to that behavioral and linguistic code.

Vega's "Aerobics" call into question the accepted norms of heterosexual attraction ("One"), sexual competitiveness ("Two"), and marriage ("Three"). The very title suggests fevered, if futile, attempts to gain control over this thing called love, or, more accurately, sex.

WRITING HISTORY ANEW

The writing collected in this anthology all fits squarely in the tradition of feminist prose, of course. But it also forms part of a national literary canon, that of contemporary Puerto Rican prose writers. These writers, men and women, are well-versed in the work of revisionist historians who are re-writing Puerto Rican history from the perspective of the oppressed classes: workers, peasants, women.[6] Much work by gifted younger writers in Puerto Rico is informed by a new understanding of the nineteenth century independence struggle, the shift of power from Spain to the U.S., the role of the working class, and the heretofore hidden, but important, role played by women in the struggle for national liberation. Rosario Ferré, for one, is particularly interested in issues of race and class, and these play a major role in her writing.[7] The particularities of class differences and the conflicts found therein, especially as these shaped Puerto Rican history after the U.S. invasion of 1898, are the raw material for many of her stories. A reading of "The Youngest Doll" is enriched by the knowledge that when political and economic sovereignty shifted from Spain to the U.S., the latter's policies—devaluation of the currency, for example—brought about the immediate demise of the coffee-growing *hacendados*. Later, the indigenous sugar cane aristocracy would meet the same fate as absentee landowners from the north consolidated their holdings into huge *latifundios*. As one class lost its economic base and went into a state of decline, another was created: a dependent professional and commercial elite whose business ethos found expression in such sayings as "time is money" and "everything has its price." Representatives of this class appear throughout Ferré's prose: the doctor who lets the female protagonist of "The Youngest Doll" suffer from a malady he could have cured, so that he could underwrite his son's medical training, is but one example. This opening tale, with its magical realism, has unusually rich and disturbing effects on the reader, not the least of which is a dispiriting awareness of time's passing on a society undergoing abrupt change. Notice the way the following sentence evokes a sense of loss: *"Por aquella época la familia vivía rodeada de un pasado que dejaba desintegrar a su alrededor con la misma impasible musicalidad con que la lámpara de cristal del comedor se desgranaba a pedazos sobre el mantel raído de la mesa."*[8] (In those days, the family was nearly ruined; they lived surrounded by a past that was breaking up around them with the same impassive musicality with which the dining room chandelier crumbled on the frayed linen cloth of the dining room table.) As the sentence unfolds we are treated to suggestions of both richness and decay, both silence and music. The referent is Puerto Rico after the U.S. invasion.

THE SHORT STORY GENRE

As in many other stories by Ferré, contradiction plays a structuring role in "The Youngest Doll." Notice how the terms "fruit, scab, scales, sex, injury, aroma, sperm" evoke sexuality's danger in a mysteriously suggestive manner, dispersing and complicating meaning by an arrangement of terms around a single event—the prawn's sting. The reader finds herself trying to pull all of these elements into *a* meaning, when in fact there is a dispersal of meaning at work. It is as if a field of various possible readings is thus created, a field which is disturbing because it is contradictory, incongruous, with suggestions of the exotic threatening to intersect the familiar, the erotic. The same incongruity is at work at the end of the story. But these contradictions are fitting; for the short story, unlike the novel, is "constructed on the basis of some contradiction, incongruity, error, contrast, etc. . . it amasses its whole weight towards the ending. Like a bomb dropped from an airplane, it must speed downwards so as to strike with its warhead full force on the target."[9]

In fact, the endings of most of these stories consist of an unsolvable conflict which comes to a head, or a paradox with no solution. Uncompromisingly open, they resist traditional closure by leaving the synthesis and interpretation squarely on the reader, who must supply a meaning or meanings in the act of reading.

Although in the quotation above, Boris Eikenbaum is defining a whole genre, the short story, his description particularly befits women's writing, especially if the belligerence implied in his "warhead" metaphor is taken literally. The acceleration of this warhead towards revenge or the unresolved contradiction in these stories is peculiarly well-suited to the fictional representation of an experience—being a woman in contemporary Puerto Rico—which is rife with contradictions. What possible space is there for the dancer in "Sleeping Beauty" for example, when social class constraints impede her movement, when she finds herself trapped in the scenario written for her by her father, her teacher, her husband, her critics? Or what of Milagros, in "Milagros, on Mercurio Street"? The reader is left in the grip of a question which cannot be answered, for the two possible subject positions, "virgin" and "whore," are not viable choices for a woman. But I would go so far as to suggest that the very term "woman" is a contradiction, for if that term is correctly seen as a cultural construct, it is both possible *and* impossible to be a "woman." It is, as Julia Kristeva says, "not in the order of being."[10] To reduce a person to her biological, "essential" or even gendered "self" as a constant subjectivity is really a kind of moral fascism. We are and are not this or that at turns, and "being" cannot be pinned down and defined once and for all.

I spoke earlier of subversion, and many of these stories are noteworthy for the way in which they subvert linguistic, cultural, gender and class codes. Some do this with generic form as well. For example, Ferré has done an admirable job of collecting and recording oral folktales which are part of Puerto Rico's rich cultural heritage. She has written versions of these oral narratives as well as fairy tales which are adapted to the Puerto Rican setting. It would not be too farfetched to state that most of her stories are, in some way or another, fairy tales. But these are not innocent, for she has, in the words of one critic, "placed bombs in the very licit genre of the fairy tale."[11] What—if not that—is taking place in Rosario Ferré's fairy tale for adults, "Pico Rico, Mandorico," with its gentle suggestion of the liberating possibilities of an all-female artistic domain (including lesbianism)? This tale undermines both compulsory heterosexuality and compulsive work, while making specific reference to a particular cultural context—Pico Rico, Puerto Rico. A creative rewriting of Christina Rosetti's "Goblin Market," the story's simplicity is deceptive.

Carmen Lugo Filippi, for her part, suggests the possibility of female collaboration as part of *and* in opposition to patriarchy's socialization of women in her story "Milagros, on Mercurio Street." The story's protagonist, Marina, helps the object of her desire, Milagros, to accept the male gaze by showing Milagros her reflected image in the mirror. When the adolescent takes this acceptance to its unexpected conclusion, Marina has to face her own complicity in these events. At the end of the story, Marina and the reader are asked to take a position as to how Milagros is to be reconstituted in society. The story is a radical questioning of the construction of identity and allows for no easy answer to the question posed. One possible reading is that in questioning her own position, Marina has advanced to a place where she can evolve and change. Milagros remains problematic.

One of the means used to make the issue of identity more fluid in this story is the construction of a narrative voice which is split. The usual comfort experienced by the reader when she reads a story told in the realist tradition is undermined as the narrative voice shifts from first person to second. The second person narrator in this story can be read as Marina's superego or as an overarching superego, an ethics of behavior, which questions—somewhat aggressively—the protagonist's motives.

The story produces in some readers a feeling of discomfort, perhaps because any "solution" to the problem of Milagros' identity seems facile given the impossibility of escape from the social. At the end of the story Milagros has freed herself from the restrictions imposed by her mother's code, but her sexuality is not therefore "free." Rather, it is perhaps entering into that peculiar form of Latino sexual repression which Latinas themselves have described so well: "(W)hile the chilliest Anglo-Saxon repression of sex pretends it simply doesn't exist, Latin repression says it's a filthy fact of life, use it for what it's worth . . . shake it in his face, wear it as a decoy. It's all over the floor and it's cold and savage. It's the hatred of the powerless, turned crooked."[12] Not exactly liberation.

These innovations in form and style allow a feminist questioning of social positionings. In reading this story, it is important not to collapse the writer and Marina, the dramatized narrator. The writer has constructed a narrative in which her protagonist speaks, thinks and imagines in such a way as to appropriate another, Milagros. The text allows us, as feminist readers, to note that even though Marina is a biological and social *woman,* she masculinizes herself *vis-à-vis* Milagros in her imagination. In so doing, she becomes a man in her social positioning with regard to Milagros. This text, by complicating the narrative voice and allowing us to question Marina's motives, suggests that the problem is not in the realm of being a biological woman. It is not a problem of essence. Rather, it lies in the possible subjective positions available to us, positions which we take up as social subjects. The ending is uncompromisingly open, and the only comfort left to us as readers is to note that Marina is questioning her role and has moved from being a person capable of exploiting Milagros in her imagination, to being a more self-conscious—perhaps even feminist?—woman.

This story, together with others included in this anthology, exemplifies a stylistic shift which took place in Latin American narrative beginning in the 1960s. This shift consisted, among other things, in writing stories that were left open, unresolved. While this is clear in "Milagros," in others ("Sleeping Beauty," "ADJ, Inc.") it takes a slightly different form. Here the author, rather than presenting a smooth, easy-to-read narrative, gives the reader instead a collection of what critics call "fictive artifacts": letters, diaries, newspaper articles, even scribbled notes which are then discarded! The reader must then put the pieces of this puzzle together into a coherent story or stories. She is forced to structure the story herself.

Attention is also called to the object the reader is holding *as object,* as something which has been constructed out of language, paper and ink; in short, as artifact. Carmen Valle turns the reader of her make-believe diary entries into a voyeur (or voyeuse), but she also allows the reader to note that these are not really diaries, but representations of diaries. When the husband in "Sleeping Beauty" crumples and discards the piece of paper on which he has been writing, the reader experiences a slight jolt, for suddenly she is distanced from the comfortable and naive belief she had been enjoying just a moment before, a belief in the "reality" of the story as told. This awareness of and calling attention to the constructed nature of writing, its "artifact-ness," is a new and radical innovation in Puerto Rican writing, though many Latin American writers were experimenting with this in the 1960s.

WOMEN AS BETRAYERS OF THE STRUGGLE?

Whenever women begin to speak of our gender oppression, the monitors of culture tell us that we must organize our priorities hierarchically. Or else the demand put to us is that we claim *an* identity. Black women are asked, for example, if they are oppressed for reasons of race, class *or* gender; or the term "triple oppression" is used to describe their situation. But these terms merely reduce the complexity of experience, for one is in the world in all of one's particularity. One is "in the world" all at once, not in pieces, with gender oppression in this square, racial oppression in this other, and so on. One's experience is of all these oppressions at once. In the case of Puerto Rico, discussions of culture and power have traditionally taken place in comparative terms: Puerto Rico (as a monolith) vis-à-vis the U.S. (as a monolith), with class, race and gender distinctions rarely appearing in this seamless story. This is especially the case in writings by elite groups. But how are women going to insert themselves into this story? Five hundred years of colonialism, including the almost one hundred years under U.S. rule, demand that the Puerto Rican writer speak this reality. And this demand weighs heavily on the writer. A good percentage of Puerto Rican literature of the twentieth century addresses this colonial situation. For there has been, and continues to be, an awareness in Puerto Rico that that island nation has been, and continues to be, threatened by U.S. cultural aggression in every form. But as Ana Lydia Vega asks: "What if one of those so-called National Values (we're supposed to defend) just happens to be sexism?"[13] In other words, women cannot and will not wait for (insert your favorite goal): national liberation, revolution, independence, socialism, etc. And if Puerto Rican women writers have suffered under U.S. colonialism *together with* men, they have also suffered *because of* the sexism of their men. Contemporary Puerto Rican women's writing speaks this reality in no uncertain terms. This writing is, then, a privileged object for understanding their particular historical circumstances. It is privileged because it is written by a group of women, all of whom are feminist, all of whom have a complex, subtle understanding of both their social context in national terms and the particularities of their situation *as women* and as writers in modern-day Puerto Rico. From within that colonial setting, they challenge classism, racism, machismo and especially marianismo—that behavioral code which elevates women to a virgin's pedestal wherein they are immobilized and kept from making their own history.

One aspect of the specificity of this social formation called modern Puerto Rico is the way the island was industrialized. The "Puerto Rican Model" is the term used in social science literature to refer to that method of development which aims to attract foreign capital investment by offering numerous tax incentives to companies willing to relocate. It is a case of capital being imported. This model was sold to the Puerto Rican public with the promise that it would "modernize" Puerto Rico. Notice how innocuous the term "modernize" sounds. This industrialization of the island along the lines of dependent capitalist development brought with it enormous and rapid social changes. For one, the rural proletariat created in the first three decades—workers in sugar cane *latifundios,* for the most part—became an urban working class. Unemployment accompanied "development," for as capital-intensive industries replaced the earlier labor-intensive factories—garment producers, mostly—which had moved to the island in search of cheap labor, a reserve army of unemployed was created. By the 1960s, many of these smaller firms had moved to southeast Asia, where labor was cheaper, and capital-intensive industries—which hired few local workers—moved in to take their place. What this meant for the working class was that even though the manufacturing sector had grown and 40 percent of the labor force had emigrated to the U.S. mainland by the end of the 1950s, unemployment continued to grow. The manufacturing sector could not absorb enough of the displaced agricultural workers to reduce unemployment.[14] The rural proletariat moved into the cities, creating a mass of workers who couldn't find work and were forced to live in shanty towns surrounding the urban areas. While women could still find work—if poorly paying and seasonal—in the garment and electronics industries, men often found themselves out of work, unable to support their families. It should be noted that with improved literacy and widespread education, women also entered the professions. But here again, they tended to be those which required "nurturing" skills: teaching, social work, secretarial work. So, while there were clearly major changes in women's labor force participation, there has been and continues to be a tension between the ideology of a traditional society and the demands of an industrial society. This tension opens up a space for questioning women's roles.

RECLAIMING A LATIN AMERICAN IDENTITY

In the 1950s, along with the development program described above, social planners and government bureaucrats managed to implant a particular kind of consciousness in Puerto Rico. Its logic ran something like this: because Puerto Rico has a special relationship to the United States, it has somehow ceased to be—properly speaking—part of Latin America. Its historically assigned role was to be a "Bridge Between Two Cultures" and a "Showcase of Democracy." This was a thinly veiled attempt to sever the island's ties to the rest of Latin America, as well as to improve the appearance of the tie between the U.S. and Puerto Rico, particularly in the face of worldwide de-colonization.

Puerto Rico does, in fact, have a particular relationship to the United States. It is a colony. While it has all the trappings of a democracy—a bicameral government, due process under the law (except for those who favor independence), federal courts—in terms of power, the relationship is clearly that of colonizer and colonized. The U.S. controls Puerto Rico politically because decisions by the island legislature can be overturned by the U.S. Congress. Although Puerto Ricans serve in the U.S. armed forces, and, like Chicanos and Blacks, die in disproportionate numbers during wars, Puerto Ricans do not vote in presidential elections. The U.S. controls Puerto Rico's economy, its currency, its mail service, its "federal" courts.

The U.S. controls all of the ideological and state apparatuses. Clearly, a strong Latin American identity would undermine U.S. control, so the propaganda machine has instilled in many Puerto Ricans the idea that their peculiar political status has separated them from their Latin American neighbors. As a result, many islanders refuse to identify as Latin Americans.

But most of Puerto Rico's writers have not been fooled by this propaganda and, to this day, they identify strongly as Latin Americans. Contemporary writers also fit squarely in the Latin American literary tradition in terms of style, technique and thematics. Moreover, several Latin American "boom" writers have taught courses in Puerto Rico. Rosario Ferré, for instance, has studied with Mario Vargas Llosa.

A particularly healthy by-product of reclaiming this Latin American identity, and ending the cultural isolation of the 1950s and 1960s, is a new willingness on the part of Puerto Rican writers to play with language, incorporating into their writing various speech styles, and engaging in formal experimentation.

"DIALOGISM" AND WOMEN'S WRITING

One of the ways in which these texts play with language is through their "dialogism." The term was coined by Mikhail Bakhtin, who posits literary language as a "living mix of varied and opposing voices."[15] Bakhtin's theory of language, simply stated, is that speakers structure meaning jointly as they speak and that the basic unit of language is not the word but the utterance-in-dialogue. Language, then, is irreducibly social and human beings are constructed out of a polyphony of voices which represent various discourses: political, religious, literary, academic, and so on. Bakhtin saw the novel as the best art form for representing this polyphony. But in recent fiction, the short story, too, has become increasingly polyphonic. In fact, this structuring of a story out of a polyphony of voices can be seen as a defining element of the newest Puerto Rican prose fiction. Luis Rafael Sánchez calls it the "corruption of the traditional text" wherein "narration has utterly ceased to limit itself to a single narrative voice."[16] Instead, the text is structured out of a multiplicity of voices. This polyphony, though not specifically feminist, can be and has been usefully appropriated by feminist writers, as they write into their texts the voices of those who have been traditionally suppressed, "raising" these voices, at times, to the level of narrator. Note the difference in tone when Marina speaks in first person and when the second person narrator intervenes; or notice the language of the "dirty tricks" agent in "ADJ, Inc." The use of fictive artifacts spoken of earlier is one way of injecting polyphony. Another is the interjection of characters' voices into the narrative voice: dialogism. Another is the acceptance of the validity of regional dialect. This multiplicity represents a major change from the work of earlier, post-war writers in Puerto Rico (and elsewhere in Latin America). For example, no longer is the narrator's voice in standard Spanish, while the characters speak a "marked," hence "lower," brand. There are no quotation marks—literal or conceptual—around characters' voices here. Instead, the narrator's speech is inflected with the subjectivity of the characters and vice-versa.

"Milagros, on Mercurio Street" is a particularly good example of Bakhtinian dialogism. The story contains shifts in voice and inflections of the narrator's speech with the emotional apparatus of the characters, as well as shifts in narrative voice in terms of person. Notice that sometimes the story is told in first person, sometimes in second, as a critical superego castigates Marina: "Yes, Milagros' hair was really a challenge for you." Examples of what Bakhtin calls "double-voiced discourse" abound in this story: witness the cinematic aspect of Marina's appropriation of the object of her desire as she writes Milagros into a Buñuelian script. Or note her use of ironically religious terms as she weaves a sexual fantasy for herself near the end of the story.

Along with dialogism—and an important manifestation of it—is "heteroglossia"; literally, many languages or codes. For Bakhtin, this linguistic stratification, based on social stratification, is at the very basis of language, and is precisely what a systematic linguistics suppresses. Heteroglossia is found in literature when "the author utilizes now one language, now another, in order to avoid giving himself up wholly to either of them; he makes use of this verbal give and take, this dialog of languages at every point in his work, in order that he may remain neutral with regard to language, a third party in a quarrel between two people (although he may be a *biased* third party)."[17]

Heteroglossia is rooted in speech diversity and class stratification. National languages are dispersed, fragmented into different codes, jargons, styles, and the author can make use of this stratification in constructing a narrative. Dispensing with the singularity of speech allows us to question the naming function, allows the author to use parody and humor to undermine certain types of language or discourses. For example, the language of beauty magazines is parodied in "Pilar, Your Curls," thus enabling the reader a critical view into the way such magazines appropriate frustrated female sexuality to their own ends, inserting women into a fantasy that masks an unpleasant reality. In this case the reference is to *el viernes social,* a particularly nasty example of the island's sexism wherein the husband goes out with his (male) friends on Friday, leaving his wife at home with the children.

It is arguable, of course, that some of these stories are not feminist because they bring about closure by placing characters into the very patriarchy they wished to escape. I'm thinking of "Pilar, Your Curls," for example, or "Diary Entry #1," or the macabre "Thirteen and a Turtle." But I would say that the very representation of the impossibility of escape from the social, the cultural, is appropriate because it validates the reader's experience—thus allowing her to obtain pleasure from the act of reading. And even though we should separate the text from our reading(s) of it, even a cursory first sally into any one of these stories yields some kind of evidence of the subversion of sexist cultural norms at work. Naming the problem is the first step toward solving it.

These stories take place in the country and the city; they are set in the past, the present and the future; they are narrated in a variety of styles, using several kinds of language— compare the density of Mayra Montero's prose with the conversational tone of Carmen Valle's pieces, for example—but in all cases they question women's assigned role, they question the codes which construct for them an untenable social position, a place called "woman," a place which is impossible to occupy.

Diana Vélez
Iowa City

NOTES

1. Elizabeth Janeway, *The Writer's Book,* Chapter 1, Helen Hull, ed. cited in Elaine Partnow, ed. *The Quotable Woman, Volume Two* (Los Angeles: Pinnacle Books, 1980), 174.

2. Herbert J. Rose, *A Handbook of Greek Mythology* (New York: E.P. Dutton, 1929), 29.

3. Rose, 30.

4. Teresa de Lauretis, "Desire in Narrative," in *Alice Doesn't: Feminism, Semiotics, Cinema* (Bloomington: Indiana University Press, 1984), 109.

5. Sigmund Freud, "The Relation of the Poet to Day-Dreaming," in *On Creativity and the Unconscious* (New York: Harper and Row, 1958), 44-54.

6. Efraín Barradas, "Palabras apalabradas: Prólogo para una antología de cuentistas puertorriqueños de hoy," in *Apalabramiento: cuentos puertorriqueños de hoy* (Hanover, N.H.: Ediciones del norte, 1983), xiii-xxxi.

7. See especially Rosario Ferré's collection of short stories entitled *Papeles de Pandora,* 2nd. ed. (México, D.F.: Joaquín Mortiz, 1979).

8. Ferré, 10.

9. Boris Ejxenbaum (or Eikenbaum), *O Henry and the Theory of the Short Story,* trans. I.R. Titunik (Ann Arbor: Michigan Slavic Contributions, University of Michigan, 1968), 4.

10. Julia Kristeva, "Woman Can Never Be Defined," in Elaine Marks and Isabelle de Courtivron, *New French Feminisms* (New York: Schocken Books, 1981), 137. The translation reads, "The belief that 'one is a woman' is almost as absurd and obscurantist as the belief that 'one is a man.' . . . a woman cannot 'be'; it is something which does not even belong in the order of *being.*"

11. Ana Lydia Vega, "de bípeda desplumada a escritora puertorriqueña con E y P machúsculas: textimonios autocensurados," in *La torre del viejo* I, 2 (julio-agosto 1984), 44-48.

12. Aurora Levins Morales, " . . . And Even Fidel Can't Change That!" in *This Bridge Called My Back: Writings by Radical Women of Color* (Watertown, MA: Persephone, 1981), 56.

13. Vega, 45.

14. Américo Badillo-Veiga, "Bread (foreign), Land (wasted), Liberty (denied)," in *NACLA* XV, 2 (March-April 1981), 17.

15. Mikhail Bakhtin, "Dialogism in the Novel," in *The Dialogic Imagination: Four Essays,* edited by Michael Holquist, translated by Caryl Emerson and Michael Holquist (Austin: University of Texas Press, 1981), xxviii.

16. Luis Rafael Sánchez, "Luis Rafael Sánchez Speaks about *Macho Camacho's Beat,*" *Review 28,* 41. Sánchez's own novel is an excellent example of this polyphony.

17. Bakhtin, 314.

Translator's Preface

The word *guanábana,* for Puerto Rican readers, calls forth an auditory image of a fruit with a green, cactus-like skin and a white, fleshy, milky, juicy interior which contains shiny black pits like those of a watermelon. A sweet, sensuous, tropical fruit, it ripens quickly and has a pungent aroma after it has been lying on the ground for only a few hours. The word, moreover—like other Puerto Rican words with indigenous origins and a "gua" prefix: *guayaba, guajataca, guabancex, guarionex*—strikes chords of recognition for the Puerto Rican reader. The prefix elicits images of indigenous resistance and the survival of that indigenous world in our collective linguistic heritage.

The word for the same object in English is *sweetsop.* Most readers will have to turn to the dictionary for that one, whereas the Puerto Rican reader comes across *guanábanas* every day—if they're in season.

Consider the symbolic importance the *guanábana,* or its aroma, has in the story "The Youngest Doll." In carrying that over—for that is what "translation" means—the translator must make a decision regarding the word. Should she go with the dictionary equivalent and its most likely negative associations for an audience which has never tasted the fruit? (I say these associations are most likely negative because "sops" are not looked upon too kindly, even if they are "sweet.") Should she leave the word in the original language and hope that its velar, bilabial and nasal sounds will make up for the loss of literal meaning? Should she translate the fruit's name into another, non-tropical fruit, knowing that tropical fruits are different from the hard little apples and such we eat up north? Tropical fruits are funkier, more sensuous as an eating experience, sweeter, more aromatic. Softer. Should she weigh down *sweetsop* with adjectives that might weaken the effect?

Another example: in number two of Ana Lydia Vega's "Three Love Aerobics," "She" gives her friend's husband an *ano nuevo,* which on a first reading might just seem like a typographical error; surely she meant *año nuevo,* New Year's. But it is precisely this double play of meaning which Ana Lydia Vega exploits to humorous effect. It is not always possible to carry that effect over into English. In the case of this sentence, one has to choose between the festive atmosphere of New Year's or the reference to sodomy.

It is a commonplace that any translation involves a loss of meaning. But it is also true that any act of writing involves loss, so the "original" text is nothing more than an ideal construct; it was never complete unto itself, if only because it, too, like the translation, is the end result of a struggle with language. Of course, writing requires intentionality, but intentionality is only one small part of writing. Any writer knows that, as much as we write in a language, the language itself writes us. So, too, is the translator written by language.

As the translator takes the text through its various revisions, from an initial transliteration to its first, second and third versions and beyond, into its "final" version, the "original" story is re-written several times. Just as readers approach the same text differently at ages six, sixteen and thirty-six, and just as this given text is really each of those readings or perhaps all of them, so, too, is the translation process one which involves change, increased subtlety of understanding, and an awareness of the dialogue in which we are engaged whenever we enter into that intimate relationship called reading.

For translation is the act of reading taken one step beyond, to that space where two languages, two cultures and various subjectivities intersect and play. It is also an act of destruction. The translator must first destroy the text as written, taking it apart piece by piece. Then the translator enters into a battle with language by cutting some things out, adding others, all in order to do a faithful re-reading of the text in a different language. For, in being faithful to the original, the translator must first kill it and make it live anew in another form. The weapon used for this act must then be hidden and a coherent, smooth narrative presented to the readers of this new text, for it is to this audience which the translator must owe her first allegiance. The new text is both an impostor and the rightful king at turns.

The translator, like all human beings, has perceptual filters—linguistic, aesthetic, historical and psychological. There, at the site of writing, she engages in a dialogue with the text as she reads it, with the original language in which it was written, and with the target language and its readers. But any dialogue is problematical. Anyone who has ever been misunderstood, or who has spent time trying to decipher just what that person meant when she said what she did, knows that communication is never a straight line between points A and B—the sender and the receiver. For the word moves through a space that is complicated, "refracted" with the intentions of others. Mikhail Bakhtin's (see Introduction) metaphor for the word as it moves towards its object reminds us of battle. He sees the word as a ray of light which, as it moves towards its object, encounters a multiplicity of resistances: contradictory or opposing statements made about that object throughout its history. And indeed, communication involves struggle, for the word is again refracted as it meets the resistance of the reader's consciousness.

The only comfort a translator can take is the knowledge that the author of the "original" text had to engage in the very same battle with language and that the reader has to take part in it as well.

D.V.

The original Spanish versions of two of the stories, "Pico Rico, Mandorico" and "Thirteen and a Turtle," are included with their English translations so bilingual readers may see Ms. Vélez's craft at work. —ed.

ROSARIO
FERRÉ

Rosario Ferré's first book, *Papeles de Pandora,* was an instant success when it was first published in 1976. She published a second, expanded edition in 1979. Other works by Ferré are: *Sitio a eros,* a collection of essays evaluating the work of several women writers; *Fabulas de la garza desangrada,* a collection of poems; and the following collections and reworkings of Puerto Rican folktales: *Cuentos de Juan Bobo, El medio pollito,* and *La mona que le pisaron la cola.* Her latest work is a novel, *Maldito Amor,* which she is in the process of translating into English.

Ferré was the founder and editor of an important literary journal, *Zona de carga y descarga.* Ferré took her Ph.D. at the University of Maryland and has taught courses in Latin American literature at the Smithsonian Institution, the University of California-Berkeley, and elsewhere. She lives in Washington, D.C.

THE
YOUNGEST
DOLL

Early in the morning the maiden aunt took her rocking chair out onto the porch facing the cane fields, as she always did whenever she woke up with the urge to make a doll. As a young woman, she had often bathed in the river, but one day when the heavy rains had fed the dragontail current, she had a soft feeling of melting snow in the marrow of her bones. With her head nestled among the black rocks' reverberations, she could hear the slamming of salty foam on the beach rolled up with the sound of waves, and she suddenly thought that her hair had poured out to sea at last. At that very moment, she felt a sharp bite in her calf. Screaming, she was pulled out of the water and, writhing in pain, was taken home on a stretcher.

The doctor who examined her assured her it was nothing, that she had probably been bitten by an angry river prawn. But days passed and the scab wouldn't heal. A month later the doctor concluded that the prawn had worked its way into the soft flesh of her calf and had nestled there to grow. He prescribed a mustard plaster so that the heat would force it out. The aunt spent a whole week with her leg covered with mustard from thigh to ankle, but when the treatment was over, they found that the ulcer had grown even larger and that it was covered with a slimy, stonelike substance that couldn't be removed without endangering the whole leg. She then resigned herself to living with the prawn permanently curled up in her calf.

She had been very beautiful, but the prawn hidden under the long, gauzy folds of her skirt stripped her of all vanity. She locked herself up in her house, refusing to see any suitors. At first she devoted herself entirely to bringing up her sister's children, dragging her enormous leg around the house quite nimbly. In those days, the family was nearly ruined; they lived surrounded by a past that was breaking up around them with the same impassive musicality with which the dining room chandelier crumbled on the frayed linen cloth of the dining room table. Her nieces adored her. She would comb their hair, bathe and feed them, and when she read them stories, they would sit around her and furtively lift the starched ruffle of her skirt so as to sniff the aroma of ripe sweetsop that oozed from her leg when it was at rest.

As the girls grew up, the aunt devoted herself to making dolls for them to play with. At first they were just plain dolls, with cotton stuffing from the gourd tree and stray buttons sewn on for eyes. As time passed, though, she began to refine her craft, gaining the respect and admiration of the whole family. The birth of a doll was always cause for a ritual celebration, which explains why it never occurred to the aunt to sell them for profit, even when the girls had grown up and the family was beginning to fall into need. The aunt had continued to increase the size of the dolls so that their height and other measurements conformed to those of each of the girls. There were nine of them, and the aunt made one doll for each per year, so it became necessary to set aside a room for the dolls alone. When the eldest turned eighteen there were one hundred and twenty-six dolls of all ages in the room. Opening the door gave the impression of entering a dovecote, or the ballroom in the Czarina's palace, or a warehouse in which someone had spread out a row of tobacco leaves to dry. But the aunt did not enter the room for any of these pleasures. Instead, she would unlatch the door and gently pick up each doll, murmuring a lullaby as she rocked it: "This is how you were when you were a year old, this is you at two, and like this at three," measuring out each year of their lives against the hollow they left in her arms.

The day the eldest had turned ten, the aunt sat down in her rocking chair facing the cane fields and never got up again. She would rock away entire days on the porch, watching the patterns of rain shift in the cane fields, coming out of her stupor only when the doctor paid a visit or whenever she awoke with the desire to make a doll. Then she would call out so that everyone in the house would come and help her. On that day, one could see the hired help making repeated trips to town like cheerful Inca messengers, bringing wax, porcelain clay, lace, needles, spools of thread of every color. While these preparations were taking place, the aunt would call the niece she had dreamt about the night before into her room and take her measurements. Then she would make a wax mask of the child's face, covering it with plaster on both sides, like a living face wrapped in two dead ones. She would draw out an endless flaxen thread of melted wax through a pinpoint on its chin. The porcelain of the hands and face was always translucent; it had an ivory tint to it that formed a great contrast with the curled whiteness of the bisque faces. For the body, the aunt would send out to the garden for twenty glossy gourds. She would hold them in one hand, and with an expert twist of her knife, would slice them up against the railing of the balcony, so that the sun and breeze would dry out the cottony *guano* brains. After a few days, she would scrape off the dried fluff with a teaspoon and, with infinite patience, feed it into the doll's mouth.

The only items the aunt would agree to use that were not made by her were the glass eyeballs. They were mailed to her from Europe in all colors, but the aunt considered them useless until she had left them submerged at the bottom of the stream for a few days, so that they could learn to recognize the slightest stirring of the prawns' antennae. Only then would she carefully rinse them in ammonia water and place them, glossy as gems and nestled in a bed of cotton, at the bottom of one of her Dutch cookie tins. The dolls were always dressed in the same way, even though the girls were growing up. She would dress the younger ones in Swiss embroidery and the older ones in silk *guipure*, and on each of their heads she would tie the same bow, wide and white and trembling like the breast of a dove.

The girls began to marry and leave home. On their wedding day, the aunt would give each of them their last doll, kissing them on the forehead and telling them with a smile, "Here is your Easter Sunday." She would reassure the grooms by explaining to them that the doll was merely a sentimental ornament, of the kind that people used to place on the lid of grand pianos in the old days. From the porch, the aunt would watch the girls walk down the staircase for the last time. They would carry a modest checkered cardboard suitcase in one hand, the other hand slipped around the waist of the exuberant doll made in their image and likeness, still wearing the same old-fashioned kid slippers and gloves, and with Valenciennes bloomers barely showing under their snowy, embroidered skirts. But the hands and faces of these new dolls looked less transparent than those of the old: they had the consistency of skim milk. This difference concealed a more subtle one: the wedding doll was never stuffed with cotton but filled with honey.

All the older girls had married and only the youngest was left at home when the doctor paid his monthly visit to the aunt, bringing along his son who had just returned from studying medicine up north. The young man lifted the starched ruffle of the aunt's skirt and looked intently at the huge, swollen ulcer which oozed a perfumed sperm from the tip of its greenish scales. He pulled out his stethoscope and listened to her carefully. The aunt thought he was listening for the breathing of the prawn to see if it was still alive, and she fondly lifted his hand and placed it on the spot where he could feel the constant movement of the creature's antennae. The young man released the ruffle and looked fixedly at his father. "You could have cured this from the start," he told him. "That's true," his father answered, "but I just wanted you to come and see the prawn that has been paying for your education these twenty years."

From then on it was the young doctor who visited the old aunt every month. His interest in the youngest was evident from the start, so the aunt was able to begin her last doll in plenty of time. He would always show up wearing a pair of brightly polished shoes, a starched collar, and an ostentatious tiepin of extravagantly poor taste. After examining the aunt, he would sit in the parlor, lean his paper silhouette against the oval frame of the chair and, each time, hand the youngest an identical bouquet of purple forget-me-nots. She would offer him ginger cookies, taking the bouquet squeamishly with the tips of her fingers as if she were handling a sea urchin turned inside out. She made up her mind to marry him because she was intrigued by his sleepy profile and also because she was deathly curious to see what the dolphin flesh was like.

On her wedding day, as she was about to leave the house, the youngest was surprised to find that the doll her aunt had given her as a wedding present was warm. As she slipped her arm around its waist, she looked at it curiously, but she quickly forgot about it, so amazed was she at the excellence of its craft. The doll's face and hands were made of the most delicate Mikado porcelain. In the doll's half-open and slightly sad smile, she recognized her full set of baby teeth. There was also another notable detail: the aunt had embedded her diamond eardrops inside the doll's pupils.

The young doctor took her off to live in town, in a square house that made one think of a cement block. Each day he made her sit out on the balcony, so that passersby would be sure to see that he had married into high society. Motionless inside her cubicle of heat, the youngest began to suspect that it wasn't only her husband's silhouette that was made of paper, but his soul as well. Her suspicions were soon confirmed. One day, he pried out the doll's eyes with the tip of his scalpel and pawned them for a fancy gold pocket watch with a long embossed chain. From then on the doll remained seated on the lid of the grand piano, but with her gaze modestly lowered.

A few months later, the doctor noticed the doll was missing from her usual place and asked the youngest what she'd done with it. A sisterhood of pious ladies had offered him a healthy sum for the porcelain hands and face, which they thought would be perfect for the image of the Veronica in the next Lenten procession.

The youngest answered that the ants had at last discovered the doll was filled with honey and, streaming over the piano, had devoured it in a single night. "Since its hands and face were of Mikado porcelain," she said, "they must have thought they were made of sugar and at this very moment they are most likely wearing down their teeth, gnawing furiously at its fingers and eyelids in some underground burrow." That night the doctor dug up all the ground around the house, to no avail.

As the years passed, the doctor became a millionaire. He had slowly acquired the whole town as his clientele, people who didn't mind paying exorbitant fees in order to see a genuine member of the extinct sugar cane aristocracy up close. The youngest went on sitting in her rocking chair on the balcony, motionless in her muslin and lace, and always with lowered eyelids. Whenever her husband's patients, draped with necklaces and feathers and carrying elaborate canes, would seat themselves beside her, shaking their self-satisfied rolls of flesh with a jingling of coins, they would notice a strange scent that would involuntarily remind them of a slowly oozing sweetsop. They would then feel an uncomfortable urge to rub their hands together as though they were paws.

There was only one thing missing from the doctor's otherwise perfect happiness. He noticed that although he was aging, the youngest still kept that same firm porcelained skin she had had when he would call on her at the big house on the plantation. One night he decided to go into her bedroom to watch her as she slept. He noticed that her chest wasn't moving. He gently placed his stethoscope over her heart and heard a distant swish of water. Then the doll lifted her eyelids, and out of the empty sockets of her eyes came the frenzied antennae of all those prawns.

TRANSLATED BY DIANA VÉLEZ AND ROSARIO FERRÉ

SLEEPING
BEAUTY

DECEMBER 1, 1973

DEAR DON FELISBERTO:

I KNOW YOU'LL BE SURPRISED TO GET THIS LETTER. I FEEL THE
ONLY DECENT THING FOR ME TO DO, IN VIEW OF WHAT'S GOING ON,
IS TO WARN YOU. IT SEEMS YOUR WIFE DOESN'T APPRECIATE WHAT
YOU'RE WORTH, A HANDSOME MAN AND RICH BESIDES. IT'S ENOUGH
TO SATISFY THE MOST DEMANDING WOMAN.

FOR A FEW WEEKS NOW, I'VE WATCHED HER GO BY THE WINDOW
OF THE BEAUTY PARLOR WHERE I WORK, ALWAYS AT THE SAME TIME.
SHE TAKES THE SERVICE ELEVATOR AND GOES UP TO THE HOTEL. I CAN
SEE YOU TURNING THE ENVELOPE AROUND TO SEE IF YOU CAN FIND
OUT MY IDENTITY, IF THERE'S A RETURN ADDRESS. BUT YOU'LL NEVER
GUESS WHO I AM; THIS CITY IS FULL OF FLEABAG HOTELS WITH
BEAUTY PARLORS ON THE LOWER LEVEL. SHE ALWAYS WEARS DARK
GLASSES AND COVERS HER HAIR WITH A KERCHIEF, BUT EVEN SO I
RECOGNIZED HER EASILY FROM THE PICTURES I'VE SEEN OF HER IN
THE PAPERS. IT'S JUST THAT I'VE ALWAYS ADMIRED HER. BEING A
BALLERINA AND AT THE SAME TIME THE WIFE OF A BUSINESS TYCOON

IS NO MEAN ACHIEVEMENT. I SAY "ADMIRED" BECAUSE I'M NOT SURE I
STILL DO. THAT BUSINESS OF GOING INTO HOTEL SERVICE ELEVATORS
DISGUISED AS A MAID SEEMS RATHER SUSPICIOUS TO ME.

IF YOU STILL CARE FOR HER, I SUGGEST YOU FIND OUT WHAT
SHE'S UP TO. SHE'S PROBABLY RISKING HER REPUTATION NEEDLESSLY.
YOU KNOW THAT A LADY'S REPUTATION IS LIKE A PANE OF GLASS, IT
SMUDGES AT THE LIGHTEST TOUCH. A LADY MUSTN'T SIMPLY BE
RESPECTABLE, SHE MUST ABOVE ALL APPEAR TO BE.

SINCERELY YOURS,
A FRIEND AND ADMIRER

She folds the letter and puts it in an envelope. Painstakingly, using her left hand, she scrawls an address on it with the
same pencil she used for the letter. Then she stretches before
the mirror and stands on her toes. She walks to the barre and
starts on her daily routine.

DECEMBER 18, 1973

DEAR DON FELISBERTO:

I HAVE NO WAY OF KNOWING WHETHER OR NOT MY LAST LETTER
REACHED YOU. IF IT DID, YOU DIDN'T TAKE IT SERIOUSLY, BECAUSE
YOUR WIFE KEEPS UP HER DAILY VISITS TO THE HOTEL. DON'T YOU
LOVE HER? IF YOU DON'T LOVE HER, WHY DID YOU MARRY HER? SHE'S
RUNNING AROUND LIKE A BITCH IN HEAT AND IT DOESN'T SEEM TO
BOTHER YOU. THE LAST TIME SHE WAS HERE I FOLLOWED HER. NOW
I'LL DO MY DUTY AND GIVE YOU THE ROOM NUMBER (7B) AND THE
HOTEL: HOTEL ELYSIUM. SHE'S THERE EVERY DAY FROM THREE TO
FIVE-THIRTY. BY THE TIME YOU GET THIS LETTER, YOU WON'T BE ABLE
TO FIND ME. DON'T BOTHER CHECKING; I QUIT MY JOB AT THE
BEAUTY PARLOR AND I'M NOT GOING BACK.

SINCERELY YOURS,
A FRIEND AND ADMIRER

She folds the letter, puts it in an envelope, writes the address and leaves it on the piano. She picks up the chalk and painstakingly dusts the tips of her slippers. Then she gets up, faces the mirror, grasps the barre with her left hand and begins her exercises.

I. *COPPELIA*

Social Column
Mundo Nuevo
April 6, 1971

Coppelia, the ballet by the famous French composer Leo Délibes, was marvelously performed here last Sunday by our very own Pavlova dance troupe. For all the Beautiful People in attendance (and there really were too many of the *crème de la crème* to mention all by name), people who appreciate quality in art, the *soirée* was proof positive that the BP's cultural life is reaching unsuspected heights. (Even at $100 a ticket there wasn't an empty seat in the house!)

Our beloved María de los Angeles Fernández, daughter of our honorable mayor Don Fabiano Fernández, performed the main role admirably. The ballet was a benefit performance for the many charitable causes supported by CARE. Elizabeth, Don Fabiano's wife, wore one of Fernando Peña's exquisite creations, done in sun-yellow with tiny feathers, which contrasted strikingly with her dark hair. There, too, were Robert Martínez and his Mary (fresh from a skiing trip to Switzerland) as well as George Ramírez and his Martha (Martha was also done up in a Peña original—I love his new look—pearl-gray egret feathers!). We also loved the theater's decorations and the pretty corsages donated by Jorge Rubinstein and his Chiqui. (Would you believe

me if I told you their son sleeps in a bed made out of a
genuine racing car? That's just one of the many fascinat-
ing things to be found in the Rubinsteins' lovely man-
sion.) Elegant Johnny Paris was there, and his Florence,
dressed in jade-colored quetzal feathers in a Mojena
original inspired by the Aztec *huipil*. (It almost seemed
as if the BP's had prearranged it, for the night was all
feathers, feathers, and more feathers!)

And, as guest star for the evening, the grand surprise,
none other than Liza Minelli, who once fell in love with
a question mark-shaped diamond brooch she saw on
Elizabeth Taylor and, since she couldn't resist it, has had
an identical one made for herself which she wears every
night on her show, as a pendant hanging from one ear.

But back to our Coppelia.

Swanhilda is a young village maiden, daughter of the
burghermeister, and she is in love with Frantz. Frantz,
however, seems uninterested. Each day he goes around
the town square to walk by the house of Doctor Coppelius, where a girl sits reading on the balcony. Swanhilda,
overcome with jealousy, goes into Doctor Coppelius'
house while he is out. She discovers that Coppelia (the
girl on the balcony) is just a porcelain doll. She places
Coppelia's body on a table and, with a tiny dollmaker's
hammer, smashes each and every one of her limbs,
leaving only a mound of gleaming dust. She dresses up
as Coppelia and hides in the doll's box, stiffening her
arms and staring straight ahead.

The brilliant waltz danced by Swanhilda posing as the
doll was the high point of the evening. María de los
Angeles would bend her arms, moving them in circles
as if they were screwed on at the elbows. Her legs went
up and down stiffly, pausing slightly before each motion
and accelerating until the hinges rotated in a frenzy.
Then she began to dance round and round, spinning
madly across the room. Both the dancer who played

Doctor Coppelius and the one who played Frantz stood looking at her, aghast. It seems María de los Angeles was improvising, and her act did not fall in with her role at all. Finally, she sprang into a monumental *jetté*, leaving the audience breathless. Leaping over the orchestra pit, she pirouetted down the carpeted aisle and, flinging open the theater doors, disappeared down the street like a twirling asterisk.

We loved this new interpretation of Coppelia despite the confusion it evidently caused among the rest of the troupe.

The BP's thunderous applause was well-deserved.

---

like a flash, her toes barely touch, barely skim the felt, flight, light, first a yellow then a gray, leaping from tile to tile her name was Carmen Merengue Papa really loved her skipping over cracks, from crack to crack break your mother's back light lightning feet dance dancing is what I love just dancing when she was Papa's lover she was about my age I remember her well Carmen Merengue the trapeze artist hurtling from one trapeze into the flying knife, the human boomerang, the female firecracker, meteorite-red hair going off around her jettisoned through the air hanging by her teeth, going round and round on a silver string, whirling, faster faster till she disappeared, dancing as if nothing mattered, whether she lived or died, pinned to the tent top by reflectors, a multi-colored wasp gyrating in the distance, the bulging eyes staring at her from below, the open mouths, the shortness of breath, the sweating brows, ants in the pants of the spectators who moved around in their seats below, when the fair was over she'd visit all the bars in town, she'd stretch her rope from bar to bar, the men would place one finger on her head and Carmen Merengue would spin around, was on my way to Ponce cut through to Humacao, wide-hipped gentlemen

cheering, clapping, she was nuts, taking advantage of her, hey
lonnie lonnie, right foot horizontal, one foot in front of the
other, her body stretched out in an arc, her right arm over her
head trying to slow the seconds that slipped by just beyond her
tiptoes, concentrating all her strength on the silk cord that

---

April 9, 1971
Academy of the Sacred Heart

Dear Don Fabiano:

I am writing on behalf of our community of sisters of the
Sacred Heart of Jesus. Our great love for your daughter, a
model student since kindergarten, requires that we write to
you today. We cannot ignore the generous help you have
provided our institution, and we have always been deeply
grateful for your concern. The recent installation of a water
heater, which serves both the live-in students and the nuns'
cells, is proof of your generosity.

Your daughter's disgraceful spectacle, dancing in a public theater and dressed in a most shameless manner, was all
over the social pages of this week's papers. We know that such
spectacles are quite common in the world of ballet, but, Señor
Fernández, are you prepared to see your daughter become
part of a world so full of danger to both body and soul? What
good would it do her to gain the world if she lost her soul?
Besides, all that tossing of legs in the air, those cleavages
down to the waist, all that leaping and legspreading, Sacred
Heart of Jesus, where will it lead? I cannot keep from you that
we had placed our highest hopes in your daughter. It was
understood that, at graduation time, she would be the recipient of our school's highest honor—our Sacred Medallion.
Perhaps you are not aware of the great prestige of this prize. It
is a holy reliquary, surrounded by tiny sunbeams. Inside the
locket is an image of our Divine Husband, covered by a

monstrance. On the other side of the locket are inscribed all the names of those students who have received our Sacred Medallion. Many of them have heard the calling; in fact most have entered our convent. Imagine our distress at seeing those photographs of María de los Angeles on the front page.

The damage has already been done and your daughter's reputation will never be the same. But you could at least keep her from persisting down this shameful path. Only if she abandons the Pavlova Company will we see fit to excuse her recent behavior and allow her to continue at our school. We beg you to forgive this saddest of letters; we would have preferred never to have written it.

Most cordially yours, in the
name of Jesus Christ our Lord,
Reverend Mother Martínez

---

like a flash, toes barely touching the suncracked pavement, leaping crack over crack, break your mother's back, Felisberto's my boyfriend, says we'll get married, Carmen Merengue would never marry, no, she'd shake her head, her white face framed by false curls, the circus left without her, she stayed in the tiny room my father rented, didn't want her to be a trapeze artist any more, wanted her to be a lady, forbade her to go to bars, tried to teach her to be a lady but she would lock herself in, practice practice all the time, blind to her surroundings, worn-out cot, chipped porcelain washbasin, one slippered foot in front of the other, lifting her leg slightly to draw circles in the air, touching the surface of a pool of water with her tiptoe, but one day the circus came, she heard the music from afar, her red curls shook, she sat on the cot and covered her ears so as not to hear, but she couldn't not hear, something tugged, tugged at her knees, at her ankles, at the tips of her dance shoes, an irresistible current pulled and pulled, the music pierced the palms of her hands, her eardrums aflame

with the clatter of hooves, she rose to look at herself in the shard
of mirror she'd hung on the wall, that's what I am, a dancer,
face framed by false curls, eyelashes loosened by the heat,
thick pancaked cheeks, falsies under my dress, and that very
day she went back

April 14, 1971

Dear Reverend Mother:

Your letter made Elizabeth and I think long and hard. We
both agreed that the best thing would be to withdraw María
de los Angeles from the Pavlova Company. The matter of her
dancing had gotten a little out of hand lately, and we had
already discussed the possibility. As you know, our daughter
is a child of artistic sensibilities, and she is also very religious.
We've often found her kneeling in her room with that same
distant, ecstatic expression that takes hold of her when she is
dancing. Our greatest hope for María de los Angeles, however, is to see her someday neither as a ballerina nor as a nun,
but rather, surrounded by loving children. That is why we beg
you to refrain from stimulating an inordinate piety in her,
Mother, at this critical time when she will be most vulnerable.

María de los Angeles will inherit a large fortune as our
only child. It truly concerns us that when we have passed
away, our daughter might fall into the hands of some heartless
scoundrel who's just out for her money. One has to protect
one's fortune even after death, as you well know, Mother, for
you yourself have to watch over the considerable assets of the
Holy Church. You and I both know that money is like water, it
flows away to sea, and I'm not about to let some hustler take
away what I had to work so hard to get.

Elizabeth and I have always loved María de los Angeles
deeply, and no one can say we weren't the happiest couple on
the island when she was born. Though boys are, of course,

more helpful later on, girls are always such a comfort, and we certainly enjoyed our daughter when she was a little girl. Mother, she was the light of our house, the apple of our eye. Later we tried to teach her how to be both kind and smart, because a loving young lady with a good education is a jewel coveted by any man, but I don't know how well we succeeded! Only when I see María de los Angeles safely married, Mother, as safe in her new home as she was in ours, with a husband to protect and look out for her, will I feel at ease.

Let me point out to you, Mother, that your suggestion that María de los Angeles might someday enter your order was totally out of place. I assure you that if this were the case, we would not be able to avoid feelings of resentment and suspicion, in spite of our sincere devotion to your cause and the affection we feel toward you. The fortune accruing to the convent, in that event, would be no *pecata minuta.*

I beg your forgiveness, Mother, for being brutally honest, but truthfulness usually preserves friendship. Rest assured that, as long as I'm alive, the convent will lack nothing. My concern for God's work is genuine, and you are his sacred workers. Had Elizabeth and I had a son as well as a daughter, you would have met no resistance from us. On the contrary, we would have welcomed the possibility of her joining you in your sacred task of ridding this world of so much sin.

Please accept a most cordial greeting from an old and trusted friend,

Fabiano Fernández

April 17, 1971
Academy of the Sacred Heart

Dear Señor Fernández:

Thank you for your recent letter. Your decision to remove María de los Angeles from the harmful environment of ballet was wise. It will be just a matter of time before she forgets the whole thing, which will then seem only a fading dream. As to your suggestion that we divert her from a pious path, with all due respect, Señor Fernández, despite your being the major benefactor of our School, you know we cannot consent to that. The calling is a gift of God; we would never dare interfere with its fulfillment. As our good Lord said in the parable of the vineyard and the works, many will be called but few chosen. If María de los Angeles herself is chosen by our Divine Husband, she must be left free to heed the calling. I understand that your worldly concerns are foremost in your mind. Seeing your daughter join our community would perhaps be heart-rending for you. But that wound, Sr. Fernández, would heal in time. We must remember that the Good Lord has us here only on loan; we're in this vale of tears only for a spell. And if you ever come to believe that your daughter was lost to this world, you will have the comfort of knowing that she was found by angels. It seems to me that her given name is surely a sign that Divine Providence has been on our side since the child was born.

Respectfully yours in the
name of Jesus Christ our Lord,
Reverend Mother Martínez

April 27, 1971

Dear Reverend Mother:

You cannot imagine the suffering we are going through. The very day we told María de los Angeles about our decision to forbid her dancing, she fell gravely ill. We brought in the best specialists to examine her, but to no avail. I don't want to burden you with our sorrow; I write you these short lines because I know you are her friend and truly care for her. I beg you to pray for her, so the Lord will bring her back to us safe and sound. She's been unconscious for ten days and nights now, on intravenous feeding, without once coming out of her coma.

Your friend,
Fabiano Fernández

II. *SLEEPING BEAUTY*

it was her birthday, she was all alone, her parents had gone for a ride in the woods on their dappled mares, she thought she'd make a tour of the castle, it was so large, she'd never done that before because something was forbidden and she couldn't remember what, she went through the hallway taking tiny steps tippytoes together in tiny slippers, going up the circular stairs tippytoes together tiny steps through the dark, couldn't see a thing but she could feel something tugging at her shoes, each time more insistently, like Moira Shearer on tippytoes tapping the floor with the tips of her toes, trying to hit the note on the nose that would remind her just what it was she was forbidden to do, but no she couldn't, she bouréed without stopping to rest, she opened door after door as she went up the spiraled steps, it seemed days she was going up and up and she never reached the top, she was tired but she couldn't stop, her shoes wouldn't let her, she finally reached the cobwebbed door at the end of the tunnel, the doorknob went round and round in the palm of her hand, her fingertip pinched, a drop of blood oozed, fell, she felt herself falling, PLAFF! everything slowly dissolving, melting around her, the horses in their stalls, their saddles on their backs, the guards against the door, the lances in their hands, the cooks, the bakers, the pheasants, the quails, the fire in the fireplace, the clock under the cobwebs, everything lay down and went to sleep around her, the palace was a huge ship rigged to set out into the great unknown, a deep wave of sleep swept over her and she slept so long her bones were thin needles floating around inside her, piercing her skin, one day she heard him from afar TATI! TATI! TATI! she recognized his voice, it was Felisberto coming, she tried to get up but the heavy gold of her dress wouldn't let her rise, dance DANCE! that's what was forbidden! Felisberto draws his face closer to mine, he kisses my cheek, is it you my prince, my love, the one I've dreamt of? You've made me wait so long! Her cheeks are warm, take those blankets off, you're stifling her, wake up my love, you'll be able to dance all you want, the hundred years are up, your parents are dead, the social commentators are dead, society ladies and nuns are dead, you'll dance forever now because you'll marry me and I'll take you far away, talk to me, I can see you tiny, as though at the bottom of a well, you're getting bigger, closer, coming up from the depths, my gold dress falls away, I feel it tugging at my toes, I'm free of it now, light, naked, moving towards you, my legs breaking through the surface, kiss me again, Felisberto, she woke up

April 29, 1971

Dear Reverend Mother:

Our daughter is safe and sound! Thanks no doubt to Divine Providence, she woke up from that sleep we thought would be fatal. While she was still unconscious, Felisberto Ortiz, a young man we'd never met, paid us a visit. He told us they had been going together for some time and that he loved her deeply. What a wily daughter we have, to be able to keep a secret from us for so long! He was with her for a while, talking to her as though she could hear everything he said. Finally he asked us to remove the heavy woolen shawls we had wrapped her in to keep the little warmth still left in her body. He went on rocking her in his arms until we saw her eyelids flutter. Then he put his face close to hers, kissed her, and Bless the Lord, María de los Angeles woke up! I couldn't believe my eyes.

To sum it all up, Mother, the day's events made us agree to the young couple's plans to be married and set up house as soon as possible. Felisberto comes from a humble background, but he's a sensible young man, with feet firmly planted on the ground. We agreed to their engagement and they'll be married within a month. Of course, it saddens us that now our daughter will never be the recipient of the Sacred Medallion, as you had so wished. But I am sure that, in spite of it all, you will share our happiness, and be genuinely pleased to see María de los Angeles dressed in white.

I am, as always,
your affectionate friend,
Fabiano Fernández

Social Column
Mundo Nuevo
January 20, 1972

Dear Beautiful People: without a doubt, the most important social event of the week was the engagement between the lovely María de los Angeles Fernández, daughter of our own Don Fabiano, and Felisberto Ortiz, that handsome young man who holds so much promise as a young executive.

María de los Angeles' parents announced that the wedding would be within a month. They are already sending out invitations, printed—where else?—at Tiffany's. So go right to it, friends, start getting yourselves together, because this promises to be the wedding of the year. It should be very interesting to see the Ten Best Dressed Men competing there with the Ten Most Elegant Ladies. The occasion will bring to the fore the contest that has been going on all year long on our irresistibly exciting little island.

The cultural life of our Beautiful People will reach unheard-of levels on that day, as our beloved Don Fabiano has announced he will lend his dazzling Italian Baroque collection to the Mater Chapel, where the wedding will be held. He has also announced that he is so happy with his daughter's choice (the groom has a Ph.D. in marketing from Boston University) that he will donate a powerful Frigid King ($200,000) to the chapel, so as to free the BP's who will attend the ceremony from those inevitable little drops, as well as suspicious little odors, of perspiration brought about by the terrible heat of our island, a heat that not only ruins good clothing, but also makes elaborate hairdos turn droopy and stringy. That is why so many wedding guests skip the church ceremony these days, despite being devout and even daily churchgoers, opting instead to greet the happy couple at the hotel receiving line, where the air conditioning is usually turned on full blast. This results in a somewhat lackluster religious ceremony. But this wedding will be unique because, for the first time in the island's history, the BP's will be able to enjoy the glitter of our Holy Mother Church wrapped in a delightful Connecticut chill.

Now, the BP's have a new group which calls itself the SAP's (Super Adorable People). They get together every Sunday for brunch to comment on the weekend's parties. Then they go to the beach and tan themselves and sip piña coladas. If you consider yourself "in" and miss these beach parties, careful, because you might just be on your way "out." Oh, I almost forgot to tell you about the most recent "in" thing among BP's who are expecting a call from the stork: you must visit the very popular Lamaze Institute, which promises a painless delivery.

For my darling daughter, so as to herald her entry into the enchanted world of brides.

(Newspaper clippings pasted by María de los Angeles' mother in her daughter's Wedding Album.)

AN IDEA FOR A SHOWER

If you've recently been invited to a shower for an intimate friend or family member and it has been stipulated that presents should be for personal use, here's an idea that will tickle the guests pink: first, buy a small wicker basket, a length of plastic rope for a clothesline and a package of clothespins. Then look for four bra and panty sets in pastel colors, two or three sets of pantyhose, a baby doll set, a pretty and bouffant haircurler coverup and two or more chiffon hairnets. Stretch out the clothesline and pin the various items of clothing to it, alternating color according to taste, until you've filled the entire clothesline. Now, fold it up, clothes and all, and place it in the basket. Wrap the basket in several yards of nylon tulle and tie it with a bow surrounded by artificial flowers. You won't believe what a big hit this novel gift will be at the party.

A BRIDE'S GRACEFUL TABLE

Despite recent changes in lifestyle and decor, brides still generally prefer traditional gifts such as silverware, stemware and china.

China is now being made of very practical and sturdy materials which make it quite resistant to wear. It also comes in all kinds of modern designs. However, these sets are just not as fine as the classic porcelain sets. Elegant china such as Limoges, Bernadot or Bavarian Franconia can be found in homes where they have been handed down from generation to generation.

Silverware comes in different designs and levels of quality, among them sterling silver, silver plate, and stainless steel. Of course, stainless is practical, but for a graceful table there is nothing like sterling.

What is known as silver plate is a special process of dipping in liquid silver. Many brides ask for Reed and Barton, as it is guaranteed for a hundred years. The stemware should match the china, and there are several fine names to choose from in stemware. Brides, depending on their budgets, tend to ask for Fostoria, St. Louis or Baccarat.

A bride who makes out her list requesting these brands will have gifts that last a lifetime. It depends on the means of her guests: they might get together and, piece by piece, get her the china set, for example. If they are of more abundant means, they will probably want to give her sterling trays, vases, pitchers, gravy servers, oil and vinegar sets, etc. These articles are the *sine qua non* of a well-set table.

WHAT MAKES FOR HAPPINESS?

A beautiful house surrounded by a lovely garden, fine furniture, rugs and draperies? Trips abroad? Clothes? Plenty of money? Jewels? Latest model cars? Perhaps you have all these and are still not happy, for happiness is not to be found in worldly goods. If you believe in God and in His word, if you are a good wife and mother, one who knows how to manage the family budget and makes her home a shelter of peace and love, if you are a good neighbor, always willing to help those in need, you will be happy indeed.

From your loving mother,
Elizabeth

(Footnotes to María de los Angeles and Felisberto's Wedding Album, written in by Elizabeth, now mother to both.)
1. Exchanging rings and vowing to love each other in Sickness and in Health.

2. Drinking Holy Wine from the Golden Wedding Chalice during the Nuptial Mass.

3. María de los Angeles in profile, with the veil spilling over her face.

4. Marching down the church aisle! What a scared little girl she was!

5. Married at last! A dream come true!

6. María de los Angeles, front shot. Veil pulled back, she smiles. A married woman!

III. *GISELLE*

dressed in white like Giselle, happy because I'm marrying him I come to you and kneel at your feet, Oh Mater! pure as an Easter lily, to beg you to stand by me this most sacred day, I place my bouquet on the red velvet stool where your foot rests, looking once again at your modest pink dress, at your light blue shawl, the twelve stars fixed in a diamond arc around your head, Mater, the perfect homemaker, here I am all dressed in white, not dressed like you but like Giselle after she buried the dagger in her chest, because she suspected Loys her lover would not go on being a simple peasant as she had thought but was going to turn into a prince with vested interests, she knew Loys would stop loving her because Giselle was very clever, she knew whenever there are vested interests love plays second fiddle, that is why Giselle killed herself or perhaps she didn't perhaps she just wanted to meet the willis, to reach them she had to go through the clumsy charade of the dagger, bury it in her chest, her back to the audience, hands legs feet thrashing around unhinged, poor Giselle lost her mind, that's what the peasants said, crazy! they cried surrounding her fallen body, but she wasn't there, she hid behind the cross in the graveyard where she put on her white willis dress, she stretched it over her frozen flesh, then she donned her dance shoes never to remove them again because her fate

*was to dance dance dance through the woods and Mater
smiled from heaven because she knew that for her dancing
and praying were one and the same, her body light as a water
clock, the Queen of Death startled to see her dance, she slid her
hand through her body, pulled it back covered with tiny drops,
Giselle had no body she was made of water, suddenly the willis
fled in panic, they heard footsteps it was Loys intent on
following Giselle, a tiny voice deep inside her warned be
careful Giselle a terrible danger stalks you, Loys always suc-
ceeds in his attempts and he's not about to let Giselle get away
from him, he's bent on finding her so as to shove a baby into
her narrow clepsydra womb, so as to take away her dewdrop
lightness, widen her hips and spread out her body so she can
never be a willis again, but no, Giselle is mistaken, Loys truly
loves her, he won't get her pregnant, he'll put on a condom
light and pink he promised next to her deathbed, he takes her
by the arm and twirls her round the altar till she faces the
guests who fill the church, then he takes her hand in his so as to
give her courage, take it easy darling it's almost over, and now
as rosy-fingered dawn colors the horizon distant churchbells
can be heard and the willis must make their retreat. They're
not angels as they had so deceitfully seemed, they're demons,
their dresses are filthy crinolines, their gossamer wings are tied
to their backs with barbed wire. And what about Giselle, what
will she do? Giselle sees the willis slipping through the trees,
disappearing like sighs, she hears them calling to her but she
knows it's too late, she cannot escape, she feels Felisberto's
hand pressing her elbow, marching her down the center of the
church aisle*

Social Column
Mundo Nuevo
February 25, 1972

Well, my friends, it seems the social event of the year
has come and gone and María de los Angeles' fabulous

wedding is now just a luminous memory lingering in the minds of the elegant people of Puerto Rico.

All the BP's showed up at the Mater Chapel to see and be seen in their gala best. The pretty bride marched down an aisle lined with a waterfall of calla lilies. The main aisle of the church, off-limits to all but the bride and groom, was covered with a carpet of pure silk, imported from Thailand for the occasion. The columns of the chapel were draped from ceiling to floor with orange blossoms ingeniously woven with wires so as to give the guests the illusion that they were entering a rustling green forest. The walls were lined with authentic Caravaggios, Riberas and Carlo Dolcis, a visual feast for the BP's eyes, avid as always for the beauty that also educates. Our very own Don Fabiano kept his promise, and María de los Angeles' wedding was no less glorious than those of the Meninas in the Palace of the Prado. Now, after the installation of the air conditioning unit, the nuns will surely never forget to pray for the souls of Don Fabiano and his family. A clever way to gain entry into the kingdom of heaven, if ever there was one!

The reception, held in the private hall of the Caribe Supper Club, was something out of *A Thousand and One Nights.* The décor was entirely Elizabeth's idea, and she is used to making her dreams come true. The theme of the evening was diamonds, and all the decorations in the ballroom were done in silver tones. Three thousand orchids flown in from Venezuela were placed on a rock crystal base imported from Tiffany's. The bridal table was all done in Waterford crystal imported from Ireland; the menus were pear-shaped silver diamonds; and even the ice cubes were diamond shaped, just to give everything the perfect touch. The wedding cake was built in the shape of the Temple of Love. The porcelain bride and groom, strikingly like María de los Angeles and her Felisberto, were placed on a path of mirrors lined with

lilies and swans of delicate pastel colors. The top layer
was crowned by the temple's pavilion, which had crystal
columns and a quartz ceiling. A tiny classic Cupid with
wings of sugar revolved around it on tiptoe, aiming his
tiny arrow at whoever approached.

The main attraction of the evening was Ivonne Coll,
singing hits like "Diamonds are Forever" and "Love is a
Many-Splendored Thing."

The bride's gown was out of this world. It was remarkable for the simplicity of its lines. Our BP's should learn
a lesson from María de los Angeles, for simplicity is
always the better part of elegance.

HELLO! I ARRIVED TODAY
NAME: Fabianito Ortiz Fernández
DATE: November 5, 1972
PLACE: Mercy Hospital; Santurce, Puerto Rico
WEIGHT: 8 lbs.
PROUD FATHER: Felisberto Ortiz
HAPPY MOTHER: María de los Angeles de Ortiz

December 7, 1972
Academy of the Sacred Heart

Dear Don Fabiano:

The birth announcement for your grandson Fabianito
just arrived. My heartfelt congratulations to the new grand-
father on this happy event. They certainly didn't waste any
time. Right on target, nine months after the wedding! A child's
birth is always to be celebrated, so I can well imagine the
party you threw for your friends, champagne and cigars all
around, right there in the hospital's waiting room. You've

been anxious for a grandson for so many years, my friend, I know this must be one of the happiest moments of your life. But don't forget, Don Fabiano, that a birth is also cause for holy rejoicing. I hope to receive an invitation to the christening soon, though my advice is to avoid having one of those pagan Roman fiestas with no holds barred which have lately become fashionable in your milieu. The important thing is that the little cherub not continue a heathen, but that the doors of heaven be opened for him.

As always,
Your devoted friend in
Jesus Christ our Lord,
Reverend Mother Martínez

December 13, 1972

Dear Reverend Mother:

Thank you for your caring letter of a week ago. Elizabeth and I are going through a difficult trial; we are both grieved and depressed. It is always a comfort to know that our close friends are standing by us at a time like this.

As one would expect, our grandson's birth was a joyous occasion. Since we thought the christening would be soon, Elizabeth had gone ahead with the arrangements. The party was to take place in the Patio de los Cupidos, in the Condado Hotel's new wing, and of course, all our friends were to have been invited. These social events are very important, Mother, not only because they serve to tighten bonds of personal loyalties, but because they are good for business. Imagine how we felt, Mother, when we got a curt note from María de los Angeles telling us to cancel the party, because she had decided not to baptize her son.

This has been a hard test for us, Mother. María de los Angeles has changed a lot since she got married, she's grown distant and hardly ever calls to say hello. But we'll always have the pleasure of her child. He's a beautiful little urchin with sea-blue eyes. Let's hope they stay that way. We'll take him to the convent one of these days so you can meet him.

Please accept our
affectionate regards,
Fabiano Fernández

December 14, 1972
Academy of the Sacred Heart

Dear María de los Angeles:

Your father wrote me of your decision not to baptize your son, and I am deeply shaken. What's wrong with you, my child? I fear you may be unhappy in your marriage and that has greatly saddened me. If you are unhappy, I can understand your trying to get through to your husband, to make him see that something is wrong. But you are being unfair if you are using your own son towards that end. Who are you to play with his salvation? Just think what would become of him if he were to die a pagan! I shudder to think of it. Remember this world is a vale of tears and you have already lived your life. Now your duty is to devote yourself heart and soul to that little cherub the good Lord has sent you. We have to think in practical terms, dear, since the world is full of unavoidable suffering. Why not accept our penance here, so as to better enjoy the life beyond? Leave aside your fancies, María de los Angeles, your ballet world filled with princes and princesses. Come off your cloud and think of your child. This is your only path now. Resign yourself, my child. The Lord will look out for you.

I embrace you, as always,
with deepest affection,
Reverend Mother Martínez

DECEMBER 20, 1973

DEAR DON FABIANO:

PLEASE EXCUSE MY LONG LAPSE IN WRITING. MY AFFECTION FOR YOU HAS ALWAYS REMAINED THE SAME, DESPITE MY LONG SILENCES, AS I TRUST YOU KNOW. YOUR GRANDSON IS HANDSOME AS CAN BE AND I TAKE PLEASURE IN HIM DAILY. WITH ALL THE PROBLEMS MARÍA AND MYSELF HAVE BEEN HAVING, THE CHILD HAS BEEN A REAL COMFORT.

DON FABIANO, I BEG YOU TO KEEP WHAT I'M ABOUT TO TELL YOU IN THE STRICTEST CONFIDENCE, OUT OF CONSIDERATION FOR ME AND SYMPATHY FOR HER. NOW I REALIZE WHAT A MISTAKE IT WAS FOR US TO HAVE MOVED TO OUR NEW HOUSE IN THE SUBURBS, A YEAR AFTER FABIANITO WAS BORN. WHEN WE WERE LIVING NEAR YOU, YOU WERE ALWAYS MY ALLY AND MY GUIDE AS TO HOW TO HANDLE MARÍA DE LOS ANGELES, HOW TO LOVINGLY LEAD HER DOWN THE RIGHT PATH, SO SHE WOULDN'T GUESS IT HAD ALL BEEN PLANNED.

YOU'LL RECALL THAT, BEFORE WE WERE MARRIED, I GAVE YOUR DAUGHTER MY WORD SHE COULD CONTINUE HER CAREER AS A DANCER. THIS WAS HER ONLY CONDITION FOR MARRIAGE, AND I HAVE KEPT MY WORD TO THE LETTER. BUT YOU DON'T KNOW THE REST OF THE STORY. A FEW DAYS AFTER OUR WEDDING, MARÍA DE LOS ANGELES INSISTED THAT MY PROMISE TO LET HER DANCE INCLUDED THE UNDERSTANDING THAT WE WOULD HAVE NO CHILDREN. SHE EXPLAINED THAT ONCE DANCERS GET PREGNANT, THEIR HIPS BROADEN AND THE PHYSIOLOGICAL CHANGE MAKES IT VERY DIFFI-CULT FOR THEM TO BECOME SUCCESSFUL BALLERINAS.

YOU CAN'T IMAGINE THE TURMOIL THIS THREW ME INTO. LOVING MARÍA DE LOS ANGELES AS I DO, I HAD ALWAYS WANTED HER TO HAVE MY CHILD. I FELT IT WAS THE ONLY WAY TO KEEP HER BY ME, DON FABIANO; PERHAPS BECAUSE I COME FROM SUCH A HUMBLE BACK-GROUND, I'VE ALWAYS HAD A TERRIBLE FEAR OF LOSING HER.

I THOUGHT THAT PERHAPS THE REASON SHE DIDN'T WANT MY CHILD WAS BECAUSE I COME FROM A HUMBLE FAMILY, AND THIS

SUSPICION HURT ME DEEPLY. BUT I WON'T ALWAYS BE POOR, DON FABIANO, I WON'T ALWAYS BE POOR. COMPARED TO YOU I GUESS I AM POOR, WITH MY MEASLY ONE HUNDRED THOUSAND IN THE BANK. BUT I'VE MADE THAT HUNDRED THOUSAND THE HARD WAY, DON FABIANO, BECAUSE FAR FROM YOUR DAUGHTER'S HAVING BEEN AN ASSET TO ME, SHE'S BEEN A WEIGHT, A DRAWBACK, AN ALBATROSS. DESPITE HER UNBECOMING REPUTATION AS A DANCER, THANKS TO MY FINANCIAL SUCCESS, NO ONE IN THIS TOWN CAN AFFORD TO SNUB US, AND WE GET INVITED TO ALL OF SAN JUAN'S MAJOR SOCIAL EVENTS.

WHEN MARÍA DE LOS ANGELES TOLD ME SHE DIDN'T WANT TO HAVE A CHILD, I REMEMBERED A CONVERSATION YOU AND I HAD HAD A FEW DAYS BEFORE THE WEDDING. YOU SAID YOU WERE GLAD YOUR DAUGHTER WAS GETTING MARRIED, BECAUSE YOU WERE SURE SHE'D FINALLY SETTLE DOWN AND MAKE HER PEACE. AND THEN YOU ADDED WITH A LAUGH THAT YOU HOPED WE WOULDN'T TAKE LONG IN GIVING YOU A GRANDSON, BECAUSE YOU NEEDED AN HEIR TO FIGHT FOR YOUR MONEY WHEN YOU WERE NO LONGER AROUND. BUT I DIDN'T FIND YOUR JOKE THE LEAST BIT FUNNY. I REMEMBER THINKING, "WHO DOES THIS MAN THINK HE'S TALKING TO? A HEALTHY STUD HE CAN MARRY HIS DAUGHTER OFF TO?" LATER I GOT OVER IT, AND I REALIZED IT WAS ALL A JOKE AND THAT YOU REALLY MEANT WELL. AFTER ALL, IT WASN'T SUCH A BAD IDEA, THAT BUSINESS OF AN HEIR; NOT A BAD IDEA AT ALL. BUT IT WOULD BE *MY* HEIR. A FEW DAYS LATER I TRIED TO CONVINCE MARÍA DE LOS ANGELES THAT WE SHOULD HAVE A CHILD. I TOLD HER I LOVED HER AND DIDN'T WANT TO LOSE HER. I WAS CONVINCED THAT A CHILD WAS THE ONLY WAY TO MAKE OUR MARRIAGE LAST. BUT WHEN SHE REFUSED DOGGEDLY, I LOST MY PATIENCE, DON FABIANO—DAMMIT, I GOT HER PREGNANT AGAINST HER WILL.

RATHER THAN BRINGING PEACE TO OUR HOME, FABIANITO WAS A CURSE TO MARÍA DE LOS ANGELES FROM THE START, AND SHE SOON ABANDONED HIM TO THE CARE OF HIS NANNY. DESPITE HER FEARS OF NOT BEING ABLE TO DANCE AGAIN, HER RECOVERY HAS BEEN REMARKABLE SINCE SHE GAVE BIRTH. WE WENT ON LIKE THIS, KEEPING A PRECARIOUS PEACE, UNTIL TWO WEEKS AGO WHEN, AS THE DEVIL WOULD HAVE IT, I TOOK HER TO SEE A FLYING TRAPEZE SHOW AT THE

ASTRODOME. IT HAD JUST COME TO TOWN AND I THOUGHT SINCE SHE HAD BEEN SO DEPRESSED, IT MIGHT CHEER HER UP. THE USUAL JUGGLERS AND STRONGMEN CAME ON, AND THEN A REDHEADED WOMAN WEARING AN AFRO WALKED INTO THE ARENA. SHE DANCED ON A TIGHTROPE UP HIGH NEAR THE TENT TOP, AND I DON'T KNOW WHY, BUT MARÍA DE LOS ANGELES WAS VERY IMPRESSED. SHE'S BEEN SURPRISINGLY ABSENT, TOTALLY WOUND UP IN HERSELF SINCE THEN. WHEN I SPEAK TO HER SHE DOESN'T ANSWER, AND I HARDLY SEE HER EXCEPT AT DINNER TIME.

TO TOP IT ALL OFF, YESTERDAY—IT'S HARD TO TELL YOU ABOUT IT, DON FABIANO—I GOT AN ANONYMOUS LETTER, THE SECOND ONE IN SEVERAL DAYS; A DISGUSTING NOTE SCRAWLED IN PENCIL. WHOEVER WROTE IT MUST BE SICK. IT IMPLIES THAT MARÍA DE LOS ANGELES MEETS REGULARLY WITH A LOVER IN A HOTEL, WHEN SHE'S SUPPOSED TO BE AT THE STUDIO.

I SUPPOSE I SHOULD BE ANGRY, DON FABIANO, BUT INSTEAD I FEEL TORN TO PIECES. THE TRUTH IS, NO MATTER WHAT SHE DOES, I'LL ALWAYS LOVE HER, I CAN'T LIVE WITHOUT HER.

TOMORROW I'LL GO AND FIND OUT WHAT'S GOING ON IN THAT HOTEL ROOM. I'M SURE IT'S ALL JUST VILE SLANDER. UNHAPPY PEOPLE CAN'T STAND TO SEE OTHER PEOPLE'S HAPPINESS. STILL, I CAN'T AVOID FEELING A SENSE OF FOREBODING. YOU KNOW A MAN CAN TAKE ANYTHING, ABSOLUTELY ANYTHING BUT THIS KIND OF INNUENDO, DON FABIANO. I'M AFRAID OF WHAT MAY HAPPEN, AND YET I FEEL I MUST GO . . . .

Suddenly he stops writing and stares blankly at the wall. He crumples the note he's been writing into a tight wad and tosses it violently into the wastepaper basket.

―――――――

The afternoon sun filters in through the window of room 7B, Hotel Elysium. It lights up the dirty venetian blinds, torn on one side, and falls in strips over the naked bodies on the sofa. The man, lying on the woman, has his head turned away.

The woman slowly caresses him, burying the fingers of her left hand in his hair. In her right hand, she holds a prayerbook from which she reads aloud. "María was a virgin in all she said, did and loved." The man stirs and mutters a few indistinct words as if he were about to wake up. The woman goes on reading in a low voice, after adjusting her breast under his ear. "Mater Admirabilis, lily of the valley and flower of the mountains, pray for us. Mater Admirabilis purer than . . . ." She shuts the prayerbook and looks fixedly at the termite-ridden woodwork of the ceiling, at the water stains on the wallpaper. She'd finally worked up enough courage to do it, and everything had turned out according to plan. She had picked the man up that very afternoon, on the corner of De Diego and Ponce de León. The Oldsmobile had pulled up and she had seen the stranger stare at her through the windshield, eyebrows arched in silent query. The man had offered her twenty-five dollars and she had accepted. She had specified the hotel and they had driven in silence. She refused to look at his face even once.

Now that it was over she felt like dancing. The man slept soundly, one arm dangling to the floor, face turned towards the sofa. She slowly slid out from under the warm body, pulled a nylon rope out of her purse and stretched it taut from the hooks she had previously put into the walls. She slipped on her dancing shoes, tied the ribbons around her ankles and leaped onto the rope. A cloud of chalk from the tips of her slippers hung for a moment in the still air. She was naked except for her exaggerated makeup: thick rouge, meteorite-red hair and huge black eyelashes. She felt now she could be herself for the first time, she could be a dancer; a second or third class dancer, but a dancer nonetheless. She began, placing one foot before the other, feeling the sun cut vainly across her ankles. She didn't even turn around when she heard the door burst open violently, but went on carefully placing one foot before the . . . .

December 27, 1974

Dear Reverend Mother Martínez:

Thank you so much for the sympathy card you sent us almost a year ago. Your words, full of comfort and wisdom, were a salve for our pain. I apologize for not finding the courage to answer you until today. To speak of painful things is always to live them over again, with gestures and words which we would like to erase but can't. There are so many things we wish had been different, Mother. Our daughter's marriage, for one. We should have gotten to know her husband better before the wedding; a neurotic and ambitious young man as it turns out, now that it's too late. Perhaps if we had been more careful, María de los Angeles would still be with us.

I apologize, Mother, I know I shouldn't speak that way about Felisberto. He's also dead, and we shouldn't bear grudges against the dead. But try as I may, I just can't bring myself to forgive him. He made María de los Angeles so unhappy, tormenting her about her dancing, throwing at her the fact that she'd never been anything but a mediocre star. And what wakes me up in the middle of the night in a cold sweat, Mother, what makes me shake with anger now that it's too late, is that he was making money on her; that he had bought the Pavlova Company, and that it was paying him good dividends. My daughter, who never needed to work a day in her life, exploited by that heartless monster.

On the day of the accident, she was in her choreographer's hotel room, working on some new dance steps for her next recital, when Felisberto barged in. According to the choreographer, he stood at the door and began to hurl insults at her, threatening to thrash her right there unless she promised she'd stop dancing for good. It had always struck me that Felisberto didn't seem to mind María de los Angeles' dancing, and when he did speak against it, it was only halfheartedly. Of course, it never occurred to me he was making money on her. At the time of the accident, however, he had just received an anonymous letter, which had made him begin to be concerned about public opinion. So that afternoon he set out to teach María de los Angeles a lesson.

The choreographer, who didn't know a thing about what was going on, stood up for María de los Angeles. He tried to force Felisberto out of the room, and Felisberto pulled out a gun. He then tried to grab María de los Angeles but stumbled, accidentally shooting her. The choreographer then struck Felisberto on the head, tragically fracturing his skull.

You can't imagine what we went through, Mother. I keep seeing my daughter on the floor of that hotel dump bleeding to death, away from her mother, away from me, who would gladly have given my life to save her. I think of the uselessness of it all, and a wave of anger chokes me. When the ambulance arrived, she was already dead. Felisberto was lying next to her on the floor. They took him to Presbyterian Hospital and he was in intensive care for two weeks, but never regained consciousness.

It's been almost a year now, Mother. There seems to be a glass wall between the memory of that image and myself; a wall that tends to fog up if I draw too near. I no longer look for answers to my questions; I've finally stopped asking them. It was God's will. It was a comfort to spare no expense at her funeral. All of high society attended the funeral mass. Elizabeth and I were both touched by such proof of our friends' loyalty. All those Beautiful People and Super Adorable People whom you always refer to a little disdainfully in your letters, Mother, aren't really so bad. Deep down inside, they're decent.

We buried María de los Angeles surrounded by her bridal veil as though by a cloud bank. She looked so beautiful, her newly-washed hair gleaming over the faded satin of her wedding dress. Those who had seen her dance remarked that she seemed to be sleeping, performing for the last time her role of Sleeping Beauty. Fabianito, of course, is with us.

If it hadn't been for our daughter's sufferings, Mother, I would almost say it was all divine justice. You remember how Elizabeth and I prayed vainly for a son, so that we could grow old in peace? The ways of God are tortuous and dark, but perhaps this tragedy wasn't all in vain. María de los Angeles was a stubborn, selfish child. She never thought of the suffering she was inflicting upon us, insisting on her career as a dancer. But God, in his infinite mercy, will always be just. He left us our little cherub, to fill the void of our daughter's ingratitude. While we're on the subject, you'll soon get an invitation to his christening. We hope you'll get permission to leave the convent to attend, because we would very much like you to be his godmother.

From now on you can rest assured the convent will want for nothing, Mother. When I die, Fabianito will still be there to look after you.

I remain, as always,
Your true friend,
Fabiano Fernández

------

that ceiling is a mess looks like smashed balls up there I told you dancing was forbidden keep insisting on it and I'll break every bone in your forbidden it's forbidden so just keep on sleep sleep sleep sleep sleep sleep sleep sleep sleep sleep wake up my love I want you to marry me I'll let you dance all you want bar to bar no please not today, you'll make me pregnant I beg you Felisberto I beg you for the sake of a mess that ceiling's a mess dancing Coppelia dancing Sleeping Beauty dancing Mater knitting white cotton booties while she waits for the savior's child to grow in her oh Lord I don't mind dying but I hate to leave my children crying just forget about being a dancer forget about it you will praise him protect him so that later on he'll protect and defend you now and forever more amen now kneel down and repeat this world is a vale of tears it's the next one that counts we must earn it by suffering not with silver trays not with silver goblets not with silver pitchers not with silver slander not with words put in your mouth with a silver spoon say yes my love say you're happy dancing Giselle but this time in smelly torn crinolines with wings tied to your back with barbed wire no I'm not happy Felisberto you betrayed me that's why I've brought you here so you can see for yourself so you can picture it all in detail my whiteface my black eyelashes loosened by sweat my thick pancaked cheeks eastsidewestside onetwothree the stained ceiling the rolling wood the venetian blinds eastsidewestside onetwothree what is money made of one day the circus came to town again and she covered her ears so as not to hear but she couldn't help it something was tugging at her ankles at her knees at the tips of her shoes eastsidewestside onetwothree something was pulling dragging her far away neither safe nor sweet nor sound María de los Angeles be still with balls sheer balls money's made with sheer balls neither recant nor resign nor content nor

---

TRANSLATED BY DIANA VÉLEZ AND ROSARIO FERRÉ

PICO RICO, MANDORICO

There were once two girls who lived by themselves in a house on the edge of town. Their names were Alicia and Elisa and they were orphans, for their mother had died and their father had left town many years before. When she was on her deathbed, their kind mother called them to her side to give them her final blessing. Her parting words to them were:

"When the two of you were born, the midwife had to use great care when she untangled you from one another, for you were so tightly wrapped around each other that it was like prying open the two halves of a shell. Be sure to always work together as one and no evil shall ever befall you."

After their mother died, the two girls took charge of the house. They were twins and their faces were like white sculptures made from the very same alabaster, so the townspeople had trouble telling them apart and soon came to call them simply "the Alisias." On hot summer days, whenever the two girls walked by them, the villagers would feel as if the icy notes of xylophones were playing gently on the surface of their skin or as if a breeze from the ocean had just whistled through the branches of the trees in the parched plaza square. At those moments, the townsfolk would find themselves irresistibly drawn to the arched doorways along the streets or to the shady carriage house eaves where they would sit and rest their heads against the cool and faded walls. Watching the patterns cut by the purple vines against the adobe, they would then close their eyes and go into their dreams once more.

But the twins rarely went beyond the wrought iron gates of their yard because they could no longer stand to see the sadness in the villagers' eyes. Most of them walked around with their heads bowed down and their eyes to the ground, never asking themselves why they were resigned to their unhappy fate, working from sunrise to sunset for the rich landowner who held most of the land in the province. At night, they would go to bed promptly, but since they had spent all day working their way around bubbling cauldrons of sticky molasses, digging their way along miles of trenches and irrigation ditches, planting their way along oceans of sugar cane that whipped across their backs in green welts, they could no longer coax the sandman and had lost all ability to sleep.

With every passing day the two sisters felt closer and closer, their affection for each other making them different somehow from other people around them. Though they were already adolescents, they continued to wear white embroidered percale dresses, their long blonde hair woven up high into crowns of braids which they held together with large silver hairpins. They earned their living doing needlework— embroidery and weaving—so they each carried a pair of scissors, sharpened metal stars that hung from their waists.

The sisters shared every secret and told each other everything, so in time they became each like the shadow of the other, in the same way that dreams reflect the soul and the soul will mirror dreams. It was so much so that if one of them drank a glass of ice water too rapidly while in the midst of her housechores, the other, even if she were six miles away, would feel a sudden cold stabbing in her throat. If, while embroidering her lace some Sunday afternoon one of them would prick her finger, the other, even if she were visiting relatives in the next town, would suddenly see a drop of blood bubble up on her fingertip.

They taught themselves French at an early age, carefully doing their lessons together over breakfast. They would sit over their huge mugs of steaming milk into which they would slowly stir exactly two aromatic drops of coffee syrup kept in an emerald green jar on the table. They delighted in practicing the alphabet forwards and backwards, finding new and interesting combinations of words that they would then write down in their notebooks. They often told each other that they would someday send those words to the Language Academy as a way of marking its demise.

They knew many domestic secrets and arts as well: how to freshen up hands after their harsh contact with garlic and onion, soaking them for five minutes in an urn filled with goat's milk; how to keep fingers nimble for embroidery by soaking them in mineral water at least eight times a day and blowing on them gently afterwards. They didn't want to suffer the same fate as the other townspeople, who, because they had worked so hard, had forgotten how to coax their sleep. Instead, the sisters would always be sure to combine their labors with unusual fantasy games that would give free play to their imaginations. They spent hours trying to guess each other's thoughts and, by playing these innocent games, they came to acquire the difficult art of getting the soul to leave the body.

One time Elisa felt the sudden prickling pain of a migraine headache coming on, so she went to her bedroom to rest. Alicia said goodbye to her and went off to the marketplace to pick up some items for their evening meal. Elisa lay flat and still on her bed with the curtains drawn tightly but she could find no relief from the searing throb in her temples. Suddenly Alicia came swooping through the skylight, percale dress trailing behind her like sea foam, arms poised in a pensive way, like a Saint Ursula popping from a painting to make her midday rounds. She walked through the darkened chamber and made her way to the bed where her sister lay. She drew close to her and slowly stroked her forehead saying:

"Alicia, my sister, tell me how much you've missed me. Kiss me on the cheek and you'll see how much better you'll feel."

Blinded by the pain, Elisa opened her eyes slowly. She smiled, for she understood her sister's intent. She pulled herself up and leaned over to kiss her sister on the cheek, whispering:

"I'm feeling better, Elisa, much better, thanks to you."

Instantly her pain was gone, but they could never be sure after that if it had been Alicia or Elisa who had gone back out the skylight afterwards.

One afternoon they were sitting just inside their porch, embroidering, weaving and sewing lace during the hottest part of the day, when they looked up to see a man on a horse approaching the house. He was dressed in black silk clothes, and he rode a pasofino horse with an English saddle. The slow clipclop of the horse's hooves left sharp, even marks on the road.

When the horseman drew close they could see he was wearing a finely woven wide-brimmed hat that hid half his face. On his shoulder sat a bronze-colored monkey making faces at the two sisters. Slung over the horse's back and strapped to the saddle was a wicker basket filled to the brim with mouth-watering fruit, harvested by the townspeople for the horseman. But his most attention-getting feature was his enormous nose, a nose that came clear to the brim of his hat.

The horseman came up to where the twins were and, letting the monkey's tail curl down onto his chest in a play of arabesques, he said to them in a deep voice:

Soo, soo, roo, soo, soothing fruit
ripe bananas, deep red cherries
passion fruit and juicy pulp.
All these goods I bring to you
chew and swallow till you're full.
Gifts are they for those girls who
promise not to cry and brood
when they see me passing through.

Alicia couldn't help but laugh at such an outlandish character, saying instead in a mocking tone:

Pico Rico, what a nose!
Who can know just where it goes?
Hand me a mop, hand me a broom.
We'll soon clean up this big old room.

But Elisa could not take her eyes off the fruit basket with its bananas, cherries and passion fruit in their deep reds, yellows and purples gleaming like jewels. She turned to her sister with tears in her eyes and begged her, please, to give her a little money, for she had suddenly gotten an irresistible urge to eat some of those fruits. When Alicia heard these words, they struck fear in her heart, for she suspected that the black-clad horseman was none other than the rich landowner, who by now owned almost all the land in the region. But she kept her silence, pretending she had not heard her sister's entreaties. In a loud voice, but more seriously this time, she repeated:

Pico Rico, what a nose!
Heaven keep us from our foes.
Wish number two
and wish number one.
Wish he'd soon be
dead and gone.

Annoyed at her sister, Elisa ran to the path where the horseman stood and, in exchange for the basket, she grabbed the scissors that hung from her waist, cut off one of her golden braids, and offered it to him with its two silver hairpins still attached.

That evening, Alicia begged her sister to please remember their mother's last words warning them to always act in unison, but Elisa ignored her and ate almost all the fruit in the basket until she was completely full. Late that night she began to complain to her sister that she couldn't sleep. Sitting by her sister's side, Alicia listened to her sing absently:

Pico Rico, far and wide
leaves a mark where others hide.
You who laugh while others perish
please return the thing I cherish.

After that night, Elisa became a workhorse, walking around with her head bowed down and her eyes to the ground, never asking herself why she was resigned to her unhappy fate, working from sunrise to sunset cleaning and waxing, polishing and shining until everything gleamed, sewing and weaving until her fingertips bled from the slightest contact with silk or linen. At bedtime she would collapse into bed, exhausted, and unbraid her hair, crying because she knew she would once again enter an endless battle with the dark forces of sleeplessness.

When she realized all her care and affection were to no avail, and that her sister was growing more distant, working her fingers to the bone, Alicia sat down to cry, just inside the porch. She knew her sister was dying and she didn't want to be there to see it. She had been sitting for some time wiping her tears on her percale dress, when she heard someone coming and a voice that sang:

Soo, soo, roo, soo, soothing fruit
ripe bananas, deep red cherries
passion fruit and juicy pulp.
All these goods I bring to you
chew and swallow till you're full.
Gifts are they for those girls who
promise not to cry and brood
when they see me passing through.

Alicia looked up and gazed at the funereal horseman. He, in turn, looked steadily at her from on high, his hat firmly placed on his head, his monkey on his left shoulder and a new basket of fruit strapped to his horse. Alicia thought that if her sister were to eat of that fruit again she might recover her ability to sleep, so she ran to her sister's side to tell her the gentleman with the fruit was there and that she would buy her some fruit if she wanted it. But once having eaten of that fruit, it became impossible to hear the horseman's voice, so Elisa told her sister she must be imagining things, that there was no one there in front of the house. Realizing her hunch was right, Alicia ran to buy some fruit so as to make her sister eat of it once more. But the horseman, guessing what she was up to, spurred his horse on and galloped away, leaving behind a cloud of dust.

That very evening, Alicia hid her braids inside a kelly green silk bonnet and set out in search of the horseman. She was willing to traipse all around the region until she found him. She set about to observe all tracks carefully, for she knew his pasofino horse left such symmetrical marks that they would be impossible to miss. When she got to a town in the east, far from where she lived, she came upon a string of deep, even cuts in the road, and she knew right away she had found the horseman.

He was dozing under a shady elm and, when Alicia saw him there without his hat on, she was able to tell for sure that he was in fact the rich landowner. She approached him silently and when she was close up she realized that he was actually a handsome man: tall, olive-complected, with hair so dark it had a bluish cast. His slow, even breathing enveloped him in an aura of peaceful stillness. Alicia felt drawn to him. But suddenly she remembered her sister's tortured breathing and her nightly battles with sleeplessness and she was over-come with anger. She was convinced that what the dark horseman wanted was to be the only one left in the region able to sleep in peace. She decided to take her revenge. She came closer to him and, in a voice that was as sad as her sister's, she said:

Pico Rico, far and wide
leaves a mark where others hide.
You who laugh while others perish
please return the thing I cherish.

He thought Elisa had come back to join him at last so he let her come close. But as soon as she drew near the monkey jumped on her and pulled off her bonnet, making her two braids fall out onto her chest. When the horseman realized his mistake, he grabbed her by the arms and tried to force her to eat of the fruit, but she resisted, keeping her mouth tightly shut. Then he began to rub the fruit against her skin, covering her from head to toe with the poisonous juices. When Alicia looked down and saw that even to the folds of her volumi-nous skirts she was soaked in cherry juice, banana pulp and the purple syrup of the passion fruit, she leaped out of his arms. In a flash, she grabbed the scissors that hung from her waist and snipped off the tip of his nose, leaving just a stump.

He grabbed his nose and howled in pain, forgetting all about Alicia, who ran home right away. Elisa was on the verge of dying when Alicia came flying through the skylight. She went over to her sister and, stroking her forehead, said gently:

"Alicia, my sister, tell me how much you've missed me. Kiss me on the cheek and you'll see how much better you'll feel."

Elisa opened her eyes slowly. Heavy with exhaustion, her limp hair splayed over the pillow, she was the picture of someone beaten by sleeplessness. When she saw her sister, she forced herself to smile and answer:

"Better, my sister, thanks to you."

Alicia leaned over to be kissed, but since her face was covered with juice, some drops inevitably fell onto her sister's lips. Elisa then avidly licked her sister's face, arms and back, which were covered with rivulets of fruit juice that looked like sparkling drops of red perspiration. When she had quenched her thirst she saw that the folds of her sister's dress were smeared with banana and passion fruit pulp and she hungrily set about eating that, too. She felt better right away and, putting her arms around her sister, she promised never to act on her own again unless both were in complete agreement. And since from that day on the rich landowner was forced to walk around with a stump for a nose, the villagers were able to recognize him even from a distance and they refused to work for him from sunrise to sunset, thus regaining that wonderful ability to fall asleep once more.

PICO RICO, MANDORICO

Alicia y Elisa vivían solas en una casa a las afueras del pueblo. Se habían quedado huérfanas al morir la madre, pues el padre había abandonado el pueblo hacía ya muchos años. Poco antes de pasar a mejor vida, la buena mujer las había mandado a llamar porque quería bendecirlas e impartirles un último consejo. Cuando las vio junto a su lecho les dijo:

—Cuando ustedes dos nacieron, la comadrona tuvo que desenredarlas con mucho cuidado, porque venían abrazadas una a la otra como dos mitades de una misma concha. Pongan mucha atención de obrar siempre de acuerdo, y yo les prometo que jamás les sucederá una desgracia.

La madre murió y las niñas se hicieron cargo de la casa. Como eran gemelas y sus perfiles parecían tallados en idénticos retablos de nieve, los habitantes muy pronto desistieron en diferenciarlas, llamándolas sencillamente "las Alisias", porque al verlas pasar por las calurosas calles del pueblo les parecía sentir como si les rozara la piel un xilófono de hielo, o como si escucharan la brisa trenzándose por entre las ramas de algún arbusto de sal. Les entraban entonces unos deseos irresistibles de sentarse debajo de los antepechos húmedos de los zaguanes, o bajo los aleros sombreados de las cocheras de las casas y, recostando la cabeza contra los muros desportillados, o contra las tapias fisuradas por las feroces raíces de la trinitaria púrpura, cerrar por fin los ojos para volver a soñar.

Casi no cruzaban los macisos portones de hierro del patio, porque les resultaba doloroso ver el desaliento en que vivían sumidos la mayor parte de los habitantes del pueblo. Cabizbajos y taciturnos, sin preguntarse jamás la causa de su resignación y de su mansedumbre, trabajaban de sol a sol en las fincas del hacendado del pueblo, propietario de casi todas las tierras de la comarca. Al anochecer se acostaban y cerraban los ojos puntualmente, pero de tanto lapachar en los mostos hediondos de las mieles que se veían obligados a espumar día a día sobre la superficie borbollante de las pailas; de tanto talar surcos y abrir zanjas de regadío por entre los callejones humeantes de las cañas; de tanto sembrar, cosechar y regar aquellas interminables llanuras de carrizales rascosos que serpenteaban sobre sus espaldas sus mil látigos verdes, habían perdido por completo la facultad de conciliar el sueño.

Cada día que pasaba las hermanas se sentían más unidas, y era como si aquel cariño las hiciera diferentes del resto del mundo. En la adolescencia, siguieron vistiendo idénticas faldas encaladas de percal blanco y peinándose las trenzas en semejantes coronas rubias, que se prendían sobre la frente con largas horquillas de plata. Porque solían ganarse el sustento con el manejo de la aguja, bordando y tejiendo manteles y rebozos, cada una llevaba siempre consigo un par de tijeras gemelas, que le colgaba del cinto como una estrella amolada.

Como eran tan leales y todo se lo consultaban y confesaban entre sí, con el tiempo cada una llegó a parecer la sombra de la otra, de la misma manera que el sueño es la sombra del alma y el alma es la sombra del sueño. Su lealtad llegó a tal punto que, si en medio de las árduas tareas hogareñas, una de ellas empinaba con demasiada prisa un vaso de agua helada, al punto la otra, aunque se encontrara a diez leguas de distancia, sentía un cuchillo de hielo rozándole la garganta; o de que si, sentada en el balcón mientras llevaba a cabo la labor del día, una se pinchaba el dedo con la aguja de tejer puntillas de encaje de bolillo o blondas de chantilly, la otra, aunque se encontrara de visita en el pueblo más cercano, veía brotarle sobre la yema del dedo una misteriosa gota de sangre.

Educándose a sí mismas con esmero, aprendieron a hablar francés desde muy niñas, practicándolo a la hora del desayuno frente a sus enormes tazones de leche tibia ligada con melao, en los que dejaban caer, vertiéndolas siempre con mucho cuidado del mismo frasco esmerilado de Jean Marie Farine, tres gotas perfumadas de tinta de café. Les entusiasmaba recitarse una a la otra el abecedario al derecho y al revés, logrando sorprendentes combinaciones de palabras que luego escribían en su cuadernillo de tapas de marmolina negra, resueltas a enviárselo algún día a los miembros de la Academia de la Lengua como acta de defunción.

Conocían, además, muchas artes y secretos caseros: la manera de purificarse las manos luego del zafio contacto con el ajo y la cebolla, remojándolas durante cinco minutos en una vasija de leche de cabra; la manera de mantener los dedos ágiles y suaves para bordar con mayor primor las sábanas de holandas, sumergiéndolos por lo menos cien veces al día en agua de alumbre y soplando luego sobre ellos otras tantas veces. Para evitar que les sucediese lo mismo que al resto de los habitantes del pueblo, que de tanto trabajar habían olvidado por completo cómo conciliar el sueño, se cuidaban de alternar siempre sus labores domésticas con juegos inverosímiles en los que ejercitaban la imaginación. Solían, por ejemplo, pasarse las horas muertas adivinándose el pensamiento, y hasta llegaron a aprender, entre juego y juego inofensivo, el difícil arte de desprenderse el ánima del cuerpo. En una ocasión Elisa, súbitamente enferma, sintió la frente acribillada por el semillero de agujas de una feroz jaqueca, y decidió retirarse a su alcoba para descansar. Alicia se despidió de ella y se marchó al mercado, en busca de algún encargo que hacía falta para la cena de aquella tarde.

Entornados los visillos de las ventanas y tendida lo más inmóvil posible sobre el lecho, Elisa no hallaba tregua para aquel dolor que le subía por las sienes en una doble llamarada insoportable. Al punto entró Alicia por el tragaluz del techo y, volando como una Santa Ursula que sale de su cuadro a la hora de la siesta para dar un paseo, la barbilla apoyada sobre una mano, el codo apoyado sobre la otra y el ruedo de sus faldas de percal rozándole los tobillos como un festón de espuma, atravesó las penumbras mortecinas del cuarto. Acercándose donde yacía su hermana, aproximó su mejilla a la suya y con un movimiento lento le pasó la mano por la frente antes de preguntarle:

—¡Alicia, Alicia! ¿No es cierto que te he hecho mucha falta? Dame un beso y verás como te alivias.

Cegada casi por el dolor, Elisa entreabrió con dificultad los párpados, pero había comprendido la broma. Esbozó entonces la sombra de una sonrisa con la comisura de los labios, se incorporó lo mejor que pudo sobre los almohadones del lecho y, dándole un beso en la mejilla, le contestó casi en un susurro, "mejor, Elisa, mejor." Al punto se sintió aliviada, pero desde aquel día ninguna de las dos estaba segura de si había sido Alicia o Elisa la que había vuelto a salir por el tragaluz del techo.

Encontrábanse una tarde las hermanas sentadas a la puerta de la casa a la hora de más bochorno, tejiendo y bordando puntillas para los rebozos de las sábanas, cuando vieron acercarse por la calzada a un caballero vestido todo de paño negro, que montaba un hermoso caballo zaíno. Traía el zaíno los cascos muy afilados y a la vez un paso muy suave y ligero, como suelen tener las monturas de paso fino, y levantaba los menudillos del piso con tanta precisión y a un compás tan exacto, que dejaba tras sí una larga hilera de heridas simétricas abiertas sobre el camino.

Llevaba el jinete un amplio sombrero de jipijapa encajado hasta las cejas, que le ocultaba la mitad del rostro, y traía un pequeño tití cobrizo encaramado sobre el hombre izquierdo, desde donde le hacía a las gemelas mil morisquetas. Sobre la grupa del zaíno llevaba una canasta de mimbre, rebozante de apetitosas frutas, cosechadas para él por los habitantes del pueblo y atada a las cinchas de su aparejo. Pero lo que más llamaba a la atención sobre su presencia era su enorme nariz, que casi tropezaba con el ala de su sombrero.

El caballero se acercó a las gemelas y, dejando que la cola del mono le cayera suelta sobre el pecho, caracoleándole allí como un rizo, les dijo con hermosa voz:

Sorsolamega la sorsolita
Vendo frutas sabrosas para las niñas:
Granadas, acerolas, algarrobas
Guanábanas de a diez reales,
A la que me mire y no llore
Yo le obsequiaré un tesoro.

Ante la presencia de tan estrambótico personaje, Alicia no pudo aguantar la risa, y le contestó con una tonadita burlona:

Pico Rico Mandorico
¿Quién te dio tamaño pico?
¡Escobilla, escobillón
Bárreme este casuchón!

Elisa, sin embargo, habíase quedado mirando aquella canasta, en la que las acerolas, las granadas, las guanábanas y los algarrobos, laqueados de rojo magenta, amarillo amaranto y verde pardo, brillaban como alhajas al sol. Volviéndose entonces hacia su hermana, le pidió con lágrimas en los ojos que le prestara diez reales porque le habían entrado unas ganas irresistibles de comer de aquellas frutas. Cuando Alicia oyó esto, estuvo a punto de que se le helara la sangre en las venas, pues sospechó que el caballero era nada menos que el hacendado, dueño de casi todas las tierras de la comarca, pero no dijo nada y, haciéndose la sorda ante el ruego de su hermana, volvió a repetir en voz alta, esta vez sin risa:

Pico Rico Mandorico
¿Quién te dio tamaño pico?
¡Saber correr, saber andar,
Aléjese de nuestro lar!

Elisa miró entonces indignada a su hermana y, descendiendo hasta la orilla del camino, se cortó una de sus trenzas rubias con las tijeras que llevaba colgadas al cinto y se la ofreció al caballero junto con varias horquillas de plata, en pago por su canasta.

Aquella noche a la hora de la cena Elisa, haciendo caso omiso de los ruegos y súplicas de Alicia, quien le imploraba que por favor pensara en las advertencias de su madre y recordara que ambas deberían de actuar siempre de acuerdo, comió hasta saciarse de aquellas frutas, vaciando la canasta casi por completo. Cuando a la madrugada comenzó a quejarse de que no podía dormir, Alicia corrió a su lado. Tendida sobre el lecho Elisa no hacía más que llorar, mientras cantaba todo el tiempo en una voz como ajena:

Pico Rico Mandorico
Tú que vas, tú que vienes
Tú que riegas los manteles
Donde el rey puso su nata
¿Qué has hecho de mi oro y plata?

Alicia le preparó aquella noche infinidad de cocimientos; la hizo beber té de yerbaluisa, té de alumbre, de lechuga y de almácigo, devanándose los sesos para encontrar algún brebaje que le permitiera dormir. Pero todo fue en vano. Elisa no hacía sino dar vueltas y más vueltas sobre el lecho, mientras cantaba en una voz como ajena:

Pico Rico Mandorico
Tú que vas, tú que vienes
Tú que riegas los manteles
Donde el rey puso su nata
¿Que has hecho de mi oro y plata?

En los días subsiguientes Elisa se convirtió en un incansable animal de trabajo. Sin preguntarse la causa de su resignación y de su mansedumbre, enceraba los pisos de tabloncillos hasta dejarlos brillantes como cintas de espejo, pulía con estropajo los balaustres del balcón y los angelotes de yeso que asomaban sus rostros mofletudos por sobre las molduras de acanto de los techos de las salas, bordaba sin descanso manteles y rebozos hasta que ya los dedos le sangraban al menor contacto con la superficie quebradiza de las puntillas de organza y de linó cristal. Al atardecer caía agotada sobre el lecho y se destrenzaba el cabello llorando, para volver a debatirse inútilmente con las mórbidas medusas del insomnio.

Al ver que todos sus mimos y sus cuidos eran inútiles y que a Elisa se le desprendía cada vez con mayor rapidez la carne de los huesos, Alicia se sentó a llorar a la puerta de la casa, porque no quería estar presente a la hora de su muerte. Haría algún tiempo que se encontraba allí, ahogando sus sollozos entre los gruesos pliegues de percal de su falda, cuando oyó que alguien se acercaba por la calzada cantando:

Sorsolamegalasorsolamega
Vendo frutas sabrosas para las niñas
Granadas, acerolas, algarrobos
Guanábanas de a diez reales,
A la que mire y no llore
Yo le obsequiaré un tesoro.

Alicia levantó la cabeza que tenía inclinada sobre la falda y se quedó mirando fijamente a aquel caballero enlutado, que a su vez la observaba atentamente desde la altura de su aparejo, el sombrero enfundado sobre la frente, el mono encaramado sobre el hombro izquierdo a una nueva canasta de frutas amarrada a las cinchas de su aparejo. Pensó entonces que si su hermana volvía a comer de aquellas frutas recobraría quizá la facultad de conciliar el sueño, y corrió a su lado para decirle que el caballero había regresado y que si quería que le comprara otra canasta. Pero como a quien hubiese comido de aquellas frutas se le hacía imposible volver a escuchar la voz del caballero, Elisa le dijo que estaba viendo visiones, que ella no oía nada y que allí frente a la casa no había nadie. Convencida entonces de que su corazonada era auténtica, corrió Alicia a comprarle al caballero su nueva canasta de frutas para obligar a su hermana a comerlas cuando éste, adivinando su intención, espueleó su montura y desapareció galopando por la calzada, arremolinado en el polvo de la tarde.

Esa misma noche Alicia se ocultó las trenzas bajo un hermoso gorro de rafia verde y salió de la casa en busca del caballero. Estaba dispuesta a caminarse la comarca de extremo a extremo para encontrarlo, y observaba con mucho detenimiento el barro de las calzadas porque sabía que el paso de su caballo era tan fino y tan exacto que sus huellas serían inconfundibles. Al llegar a uno de los pueblos más retirados del este, observó una larga hilera de heridas simétricas abiertas sobre el camino y, siguiéndolas sin detenerse siquiera a respirar, dio por fin con el caballero.

Lo encontró profundamente dormido a la sombra de una ceiba y, al verlo por primera vez sin sombrero, Alicia pudo comprobar que en efecto se trataba del hacendado del pueblo. Acercándose sigilosamente a él, no pudo menos que admirarse ante su hermosura: tenía la tez muy blanca y el cabello muy negro, laqueado con diamantina azul, a la placidez de su respiración en el sueño lo envolvía en un vaho de paz. Alicia recordó de pronto la torturada respiración de Elisa, mientras luchaba noche a noche con las feroces escolopendras del insomnio, y se sintió invadida por la ira. Convencida de que lo que el caballero quería era llegar a ser el único habitante de la comarca en poder conciliar el sueño, decidió vengarse. Se acercó entonces al caballero, e imitando la triste voz de su hermana, lo despertó diciendo:

Pico Rico Mandorico
Tú que vas, tú que vienes
Tú que riegas los manteles
Donde el rey puso su nata
¿Qué has hecho de mi oro y plata?

Creyéndose que era Elisa, que había por fin venido a reunírsele, el caballero le permitió que se le acercara, pero no bien Alicia se encontró a su lado, el tití se abalanzó sobre ella y le arrebató de un tirón el gorro de rafia de la cabeza, cayéndole ambas trenzas sobre el pecho. Cuando el caballero se dio cuenta del engaño, agarró a Alicia entre sus brazos e intentó obligarla a comer de las frutas, pero Alicia atrancó los dientes con todas sus fuerzas. Comenzó este entonces a estrujarle las granadas y las acerolas por todo el cuerpo, hasta embadurnarla con su jugo venenoso por todas partes. Cuando Alicia se vio los brazos, los hombros y hasta las piernas empapadas de jugo bermejo y los gruesos pliegues de su falda igualmente enbarrados de pulpa de guanábanas y de pulpa de algarrobo, se zafó con violencia de los brazos del caballero y, empuñando con decisión las tijeras que le colgaban del cinto, de un sólo tijeretazo le cercenó la punta de la nariz, dejándosela tuca.

Cuando el caballero sintió aquel dolor tan intenso, no le quedó más remedio que soltar a Alicia y ésta al punto salió corriendo hacia su casa. Sentíase ya Elisa a las puertas de la muerte cuando Alicia entró volando a su cuarto por el tragaluz del techo. Al llegar junto a su hermana, le pasó lentamente la mano por la frente antes de preguntarle:

—¡Alicia, Alicia! ¿No es cierto que te he hecho mucha falta? Dame un beso y verás como te alivias.

Elisa entreabrió con dificultad los ojos. Sentía ya sobre los párpados dos gruesas lajas de plomo y sus cabellos destrenzados se derramaban en desorden sobre los almohadones como las mórbidas medusas del insomnio. Al ver a su hermana, hizo un gran esfuerzo y, esbozando una sonrisa exangüe con la comisura de los labios, le contestó, casi como en un suspiro:

"Mejor, Elisa, mejor."

Alicia se inclinó entonces sobre el lecho y le ofreció a su hermana la mejilla para que le diera un beso, pero como la llevaba empapada de jugo de granada y de jugo de acerola, algunas de aquellas gotas fueron a caer inevitablemente sobre los labios de Elisa. Esta comenzó entonces a lamer con avidez el rostro, los brazos a las espaldas de su hermana, por donde el jugo de las frutas se deslizaba a chorros, como un espeso sudor bermejo. Cuando hubo saciado su sed, advirtió que Alicia llevaba los gruesos pliegues de su falda recargados de pulpa de guanábana y de pulpa de algarrobo y comió también de estas vorazmente. En seguida se sintió mejor y, estrechando entre sus brazos a su hermana, le prometió no volver a actuar jamás sin estar primero de acuerdo con ella. Y como en adelante los habitantes del pueblo pudieron reconocer al hacendado, a distancia y fácilmente, porque éste se veía condenado a pasearse por la comarca con la nariz tuca, se dieron cuenta de lo absurdo de su resignación y de su mansedumbre y se negaron a trabajar para él de sol a sol, recobrando al punto la maravillosa facultad de conciliar el sueño.

CARMEN
LUGO
FILIPPI

Photo: Aida E. Vázquez

Carmen Lugo Filippi was born in Ponce, Puerto Rico. She is a professor of French at the University of Puerto Rico. Together with Ana Lydia Vega, she is co-author of the bestseller *Vírgenes y mártires*. She has also co-authored a French language text for Spanish speakers, *Le francais vécu*.

MILAGROS, ON MERCURIO STREET

After working in those elegant San Juan salons with stylists used to entering competitions in New York or Paris every year, I had to admit my new environment depressed me a little. But I tried to adjust to these surroundings by telling myself that it was certainly better than working for someone else and having to take orders all day for a measly salary, plus tips, that hardly made up for those rough Friday evening shifts and those horrendous Saturday morning invasions by pseudo-elegant ladies in search of their lost youth. It was the tourists I found most amusing, especially the Spaniards. Juan would always pass them on to me because, as he put it, I had just the right touch. Let's just say the only person there with three years of college under her belt, and some travel time abroad, was yours truly—all of which gave me a certain advantage among Juan's ten assistants. Of course this edge had brought about some resentment among the girls, but I had managed to dissipate it with a smile and a friendly gesture or two. What finally calmed them down, once and for all, was probably the tone of sincerity I used whenever I'd tell them three years of college hardly equips anyone to inhabit the highest spheres of the intellectual realm, much less if you've never even finished your studies for a B.A. I would reduce their level of frustration by assuring them that many female graduates with diplomas hot off the press were working as stewardesses or waitresses just to pay the bills. Honey, you're better off with a couple of courses in hairstyling than with three years of literature . . . that's how I'd keep them quiet so they'd leave me to chew my own frustration, which there was plenty of, believe you me.

Yes, because I had never forgiven myself for suddenly giving up my studies to marry Freddy. I should have gone on for the B.A., should have gone on writing, should have . . . it went on and on. Everybody told me I had such promise when I won second prize in that writing contest. I still ask myself how the hell I could have been so blind. It was probably my fear of becoming an old maid. The ones I knew horrified me, especially when I thought of my poor aunt caring for my grandmother and Uncle Manuel year in and year out. Oh please, anything but that. The fact is, when Freddy entered the picture and asked me to marry him, I fell for it. He promised me castles in the air: next year he'd be transferred and we'd live on the Torrejón army base near Madrid. Travel! Adventure! With France a hop, skip and a jump away I'd get to practice the little French I'd studied. And with Italy so close I could always . . . .

But I never got to live out these dreams because Freddy couldn't leave Madrid while he was in the army and I became pregnant right away. By the time my daughter turned one, I was close to having a nervous breakdown. I just couldn't take the daily routine at home; I needed to get out and talk to other people, especially to someone who might understand what I was feeling. Freddy's conversation consisted of stories about his buddies on the base, and even that was only when he was in the mood to talk. Millie, the girl who used to cut my hair, took pity on me and asked me if I'd give her a hand shampooing people's hair. That's how I got my start in the hairstyling business. And it turned out I had quite a knack for it. I'd get all wrapped up in dreaming up and trying out the most elaborate hairdos and Millie would go on and on about how she'd never come across anyone with such talent. She forced me to sign up for a short course on makeup and styling. And she didn't throw her money away, either: I graduated first in the class.

That was when my career really took off. I was working in an elegant salon on Madrid's Goya Avenue. All the girls working there were impressed by my skills—the polyglot, they called me. I'd wow them with my ability to deal with both American and French tourists. I had never felt as important as I did then.

My marriage was not doing too well, but at least my work made up for having a husband whose idea of a good time was going to the races and the officers' club.

One day he came around with some story about a transfer to Alabama, and then I knew for sure I didn't give a damn about his military career. I packed my things, grabbed the kid, and said so long—which eventually turned into a permanent farewell. It was the best thing for all of us.

Working at Juan's helped get my mind off things. Sometimes the customers would amuse me, with their false airs of superiority, perfect clowns trying to act like *grandes dames*. I could spot them a mile away and would give myself the pleasure of beating them at their own game. An innocently cutting remark, a discreet criticism and finally, zap! I'd cut them down to size by correcting their grammar. I was so good at bringing them down to earth that even Juan was impressed by my *savoir faire*. If they asked for a "fab setting," I would arch my brows and, enunciating perfectly, ask solicitously if they wanted the protein-enriched fixative for dry or oily hair or, leaning over like a model in a Miss Clairol ad, I'd point to the "natural aerosol" just in that day. It never failed. They'd leave me generous tips of fifteen percent or more, glancing at me in furtive admiration as they left.

I would have kept on working there if it hadn't been for my mother, who came up with the idea that I could set up shop in her house. She kept up her litany of "Just try it, try it, honey. You'll do well here in Ponce. There's a sure-fire clientele and you won't have to pay rent. It'll go well for you."

That's how I got started here on Mercurio Street. I did it more for Mother than for myself. After two weeks I was all set for business on the ground floor of her modest home. The place actually looked kind of cute: walls lined with collages of haircuts and styles I had designed myself and three identical dryers lined up in front of one huge mirror with a simple frame. (I've always detested those cheap baroque ones they sell at Woolworth's.)

I didn't have to wait long for clients. Just before graduation I had a full house for three days straight. There was an unending stream of ninth-grade girls with their respective mothers. Some came in for perms, others for cuts, and a good number came in to have their hair straightened.

The place was a little modest, with a clientele that consisted of four or five nurses, a couple of schoolteachers, secretaries and a factory worker or two. I had no major complaints because I was pulling in a little money without knocking myself out too much, and my mother was around to help with babysitting. I was finally getting through that lonely spell. I put away every penny I could save for my tuition. Those days I thought only of going back to school.

It was just around that time that I saw Milagros for the first time. I recall it vividly. It was like watching one of those black and white Spanish movies, you know those somber ones that have the story taking place in a one-horse town . . . a willowy protagonist with long tresses walking along slowly . . . suddenly, the camera zooms in—a perfect close-up—then slowly glides over her facial features, focusing especially on her languid, distant eyes.

Every day, at four o'clock sharp, she would walk by on her way home from school. Impassive in her maroon and beige uniform, she looked like she wouldn't crack a smile if the pope himself were to appear. Her movement down the street was a study in exactitude: shoulders perfectly balanced, head held high, arms swinging gently in harmonious rhythm.

I would sit there watching her walk along. Film, literature and music would join forces to elicit in me a series of ever-changing images and impressions of what seemed a mysterious, and somewhat exotic, creature—completely out of place on that mundane and nondescript street. I would sit there imagining that girl walking into Juan's salon unannounced and causing quite a stir. Envious glances from dieting ladies and frenzied offers from Juan of handing her the world on a silver platter if only she'd agree to model his latest hairdo in New York.

Yes, Milagros' hair was really a challenge for you. You would fantasize about possible hairdos you could effect on her, real works of art fit for the pages of *Hair and Style* or *Jours de France.* That's why, one afternoon when you couldn't stand it any more, you brought up her name in a confidential tone while you were chatting with Doña Fina:

"Gee, isn't it a shame about Milagros' hair? If she doesn't take better care of it, she might wind up losing it."

And Doña Fina, rather harmless as gossips go, came back with:

"Oh, it's all her mother's fault, you know, Marina, she won't allow the girl to cut off even an inch of it . . . you have no idea how fanatical those holy rollers can get."

That's when you realized why she wore no makeup and, even in midsummer, went around in blouses straight out of a convent. So you probed a little more and Doña Fina, a Baptist, but not too far gone, gave you their entire family history before you could bat an eyelash.

"Keep an eye out for them; they go by at seven on the dot every day on their way to church."

So of course you were right there at your post, watching from your balcony as they made their twilight pilgrimage that evening. The mother stumbled along, clutching a huge Bible under her arm. Her apocalyptic seriousness contrasted sharply with the grotesquely humorous figure she cut as she literally dragged along a girl of about five years of age whom you took to be Milagros' sister because of their resemblance. Milagros walked along with her usual gait, about a foot behind the other two. She was carrying a slim volume—hymns or prayers, perhaps? That solemn figure cast you into a whirlwind of reminiscences of your college student days, when your regular attendance at the university film society's screenings allowed you to feed your sophomoric self-image of serious intellectual immersed in film: Buñuel, Bardem, Pasolini and who knows what others.

"A typically Buñuel scene," you declared that Tuesday, surrounding yourself in the self-importance granted by your superior cinematographic knowledge and your past participation in pretentious little gatherings—informal round tables—held in the Humanities hallway by your peers. Oh how well you remember them! Stretched out at the far end of the hallway, assuming Olympic attitudes of jaded cynics who have seen it all. For a split second you almost wished they were there with you, watching these figures moving along, so you could all sit and elaborate the most abstruse existentialist theories afterwards. But that day you were there all by yourself.

From that Tuesday on, you took it upon yourself to watch them closely each day as they walked by. You began to observe and add subtle details to your already formed image of the girl. You noted, for example, that Milagros began to lag behind, making her mother stop and wait for her to catch up before crossing the intersection at the corner. You also started to see small changes in the girl's clothing: a v-necked blouse cut a little low, a slightly tighter skirt and one day a pair of cheap but flashy sandals.

I finally couldn't contain my curiosity, and I followed them, at a distance, with the secret purpose of mixing in with the crowd of churchgoers. I wanted to see these super-punctual women performing their secret rituals. In my over-worked imagination I could see them going into trances and shaking in religious possession. But I had a hard time pictur-ing Milagros in such a vulgar state of hysteria.

The things I saw that evening made a big impression on me. So much so that afterwards—to my own amazement—I would remember the scene over and over again. Most of all, I remembered that loud "Send down your fire, Lord, send it on down!" suddenly drowned out by the unexpected shaking of a tambourine whose tinkling lasted a few more seconds as a kind of background music to the sporadic shouts of "Halle-lujah, Lord" and "Glory be" sprinkled with occasional moans and sighs. Milagros' mother was changing right before my eyes: growing taller and taller (was she standing on tiptoes?) as she jabbed her arms in all directions with such force that I feared a few times she would knock Milagros down onto the bench. But what really knocked me out, and even distracted me because of its contrast, was the image of the girl sitting there majestically watching the spectacle, shaking her head almost imperceptibly, in a magnificent gesture of indifference.

A couple of days later, on a Saturday, I had quite a surprise in store for me. There they were, the two of them, waiting for me by the door of the salon. The mother wasted no time in telling me that the girl was losing her hair and she urgently needed one of those treatments she knew I gave.

I carefully examined the sphinx's locks and pronounced the problem acute psoriasis. The treatment would take three weeks since the quantity of hair would make massaging her scalp more difficult, and each time I'd have to put on a heating cap it would be a real odyssey getting those beautiful tresses to stay in place. Since I was strictly forbidden to cut off even an inch of hair, it would have made the treatments even more tedious, had it not been for the fact that it would also give me the opportunity to observe up close the expression on that little Madonna's face. Was it possible that she was just slightly retarded and only had the air of a big city model?

She didn't utter a word while her mother was there. She just sat gazing fixedly at her own image in the large mirror, almost without blinking.

She returned the following Tuesday for her first treatment. This time she was alone. Wearing her school uniform, she looked a little paler than usual. I greeted her warmly and asked, "How's school?" to which she responded with a laconic, "Fine." I ignored her curtness and started my monologue about how she should take better care of her hair, warning her of the danger of losing it altogether if she didn't get it trimmed once in a while. "It's just like a plant, girl, you have to prune it now and again," a cliché that somehow seemed appropriate to me. I approached her from behind and gathered up her hair with a professional flourish, winding it around and piling it high on her head. "See how cute you look this way, just like a movie star," I said as I put in one of those plastic combs with pink and yellow forget-me-nots. She was clearly moved; she leaned forward and stared into the mirror, unsure the image was hers. Then she smiled at me and laughed, not knowing what to say. I got her a stack of magazines with various hairdos in them and, as I put on her heating cap, suggested to her that she pick out the one she liked the most. "I'm not allowed to cut my hair," she stated dryly. But despite her curtness, she buried herself in the magazines.

During the third treatment, Milagros seemed a little more open. She even asked me for magazines and romance comics, literature which is essential in any beauty salon. I remember handing her a copy of *Vanidades* which had a long article about how to apply makeup according to the shape of your face. Every once in a while, she would interrupt her reading to ask me about some term or another. The careful way in which she formulated her questions bespoke an incisive and clear mind. I took the opportunity to ask her what she planned to do after graduation, but her answers were evasive. She buried her head in the magazine's images and didn't say a word for the longest time.

One day—I don't recall whether it was a Tuesday or a Thursday—Milagros came to the salon around three o'clock. I had no customers that day, the usual mid-month slump, so I left her there by herself while I went to the supply warehouse to pick up a box of placenta conditioners.

When I got back I was surprised to hear music since I hadn't left the radio on. I went in quietly and there was Milagros, with her back to me in front of the radio, which she had placed on an improvised shelf near the back door. It was a pleasant surprise to hear her murmuring the words of the current hit to herself: "You're just yesterday's paper / even though your story made the front page." But I was even more tickled to see her moving rhythmically as she sang in a falsetto, "Why read a paper that's a day old? / Why read a paper that's a day cold?" I didn't interrupt her performance; on the contrary, I let her continue her gyrations. But when she caught sight of me she was embarrassed. I made believe I hadn't noticed and continued mechanically putting away the supplies. With a gesture of indifference I indicated to her that she could go on listening to the music. It was no use. Even the final riff of the song failed to pull her out of her suddenly distant manner. Her unexpected rigidity saddened me.

The results of the treatments were successful, and she gave me a grateful farewell one Thursday afternoon. She walked out of the salon with a brown paper bag full of magazines under her arm.

Each day after school she would stop by and say hello. Toward the end of November, I noticed she was coming by at around five. I figured it was probably due to some change in her schedule and thought no more of it. Those were busy days for me, surrounded as I was by patterns and sewing fabric, as my daughter was going to be the flower girl in my cousin's wedding.

That first Monday in December I ran some errands for my cousin, picking up the bridesmaids' hats and some other decorations for the tables at the reception. I followed the shoemakers' dictum, for my own good, and never opened the salon on Mondays. Between one errand and another I got home at around five. As soon as I turned the corner I knew something unusual was up. I could make out four or five neighbors gathered in front of Doña Fina's house. I could tell by their angry gestures that something big was cooking. I walked straight over and I must say they welcomed me into their inner sanctum with expressions that were . . . malevolent? conspiratorial? piously concerned? Doña Fina laid it all out without my having to say a word.

"Honey, it was around four. I was busy raking up those damned *quenepa* leaves when a patrol car pulled up with his lights on. And I start wondering who got mugged? You know that's the first thing you think of these days, Marinita, what with all this crime and all . . . . The police car pulled up right in front of the holy rollers' house and I saw my nephew Rada, you've seen him, the one who's a cop. And who do you think they pull out of the patrol car? Milagros, honey. Milagros. I thought she'd been in an accident so I ran over to see if I could lend a hand. But honey, I still can't believe what I saw. I mean, I stopped dead in my tracks. She didn't look anything like the Milagros I knew—with all that makeup smeared all over her face. They took her inside, and I followed them in because Doña Luisa was still standing there by the door with her mouth hanging open. Rada gestured to me to leave. Well you should have heard the racket that broke out then! You could hear the shouting way down on Reina Street. I never dreamed Doña Luisa knew so many dirty words because she called that girl everything from filthy whore on down . . . it makes my ears burn to repeat them, even daughter of Satan, she called her.

"I came back here to wait for Rada. You know how he always stops in to have some coffee. So I sat down on the

porch and waited, and soon enough he showed up, all nervous and flushed. The story he told me! Still waters run deep, I
always say. You can't trust anyone. That Milagros, such a quiet,
serious girl and look at what she was up to after school.
Nothing less than taking her clothes off in one of those
roadside bars near Guayanilla. That stuff they call striptease
. . . taking her clothes off, no less!"

She took a deep breath and looked at each of us in turn,
clearly enjoying our confusion, our disbelief and the expressions of supplication on our faces. She took pleasure in
stretching out her story, she savored the transition that would
give us entry into the sinful den, that magical phrase, her open
sesame, the sign and symbol that would allow us to witness
the secret ritual of that unknown priestess.

"Rada went over to Guayanilla in his patrol car because
someone had reported the place as a club where a bunch of
dirty old men from Ponce got together to watch young girls
strip. He and another cop caught them all red-handed
because they went in very quietly. Everything was dark in
there, the only thing you could see was one of those revolving
strobe lights and a big table in the middle of the place. Of
course there had to be a light in there, that's where they did all
their filth. Sure they were going to have a light, and a big one,
at that. All those dirty old men worked up and drooling, with
just a little music tinkling in the background and some drinks
. . . bunch of degenerates. There were even some doctors
and lawyers there."

There's no stopping Doña Fina now, she goes on describing the scene while you, Marina, begin to recreate each
detail in your own mind, fascinated as you are before that
abysmal world that's taking shape before you. You give yourself over to those ever-changing images, and a kind of visual
vertigo forces you to lean against a tree so that you can
maintain some order in those scenes and images that come
pouring forth all in a jumble.

There's Rada slipping in through the beaded curtain. He gets in with no trouble, but it's so dark he has to feel his way along the walls. Farther in, he sees another beaded curtain just like the first one. He separates the strands quietly so as to avoid attracting any attention and pokes his chubby face into the space. Not a single voice is heard. Just loud panting rasping against a sinuous melody that slithers out in slow motion. Fresh layers of smoke accumulate around a spot in the distance that appears and disappears by turns, as the light turns and sheds its cold blue light ever so briefly. Rada moves towards the group and goes in just when the beam of light hits a mass of pale, vibrant flesh that follows the twists and turns of each note put out by the saxophone. He can no longer take his eyes away from that improvised altar, and, hypnotized just like the sexagenarian acolytes around him, he awaits the return of the light shed by the strobe. The strobe light revolves ever so slowly, caressing that tiny foot with its rays just as the cymbals break out in sound over and over again. That milky mass of flesh begins its sensuous gyrations while the melody sounds its refrain once more. This time the indiscreet light pursues those convulsive movements and Rada gets excited as he watches the serpentine figure bend way over and, with a studied slowness, display two perfect globes. Below them, the flat geography of a perfect torso. Then, rising slowly, her back to the audience, the sinuous cat lifts her arms to her head, awaiting the final drum roll, the one that tells her when to pull out the comb holding her hair, a movement that will allow her to twirl around, revealing her nudity ever so briefly. The ragged breathing in the room stops for one perfect moment and a hungry conspiracy of looks pierces the helpless image of a nymph goddess. There, before Rada's astonished eyes, is Milagros. He blinks in disbelief and rubs his eyes, only to see those milky thighs still there before him, covered with strands of hair interspersed with pink and yellow forget-me-nots. Completely removed from the titters and heavy breathing around him, unaware of the half-uttered supplications of those libidinous elders, oblivious to the insistent trumpet blasts that sustain Milagros' upright posture, Rada stares at those tiny breasts. The clashing cymbals snap him back to reality.

That's probably what it was like, Marina. The rite was over and there was a standing ovation for Milagros despite Rada's indignant shouts; Rada, who, reclaiming his duty, was pulling his gun out and ordering them to turn the lights back on.

"That's when all hell broke loose, Marinita. They all tried to scramble out but since they were mostly old farts it was no big deal rounding them up. Some of the lawyers tried to scare Rada by mentioning friends of theirs who were judges. Anyway, we all know nothing ever comes of it for their kind. Around here these things are taken care of if you've got money and connections. And since Rada didn't want to hurt Milagros, he just gave them a warning and brought the holy roller home to her mother. He's a prince, that Rada."

You look out at that quiet house at the end of the street and wonder what part of it Milagros is huddled in right now, aching from her bruises, awaiting the inevitable swelling and black and blue marks that will multiply as darkness falls tonight.

You toss and turn all night and wake up to the persistent image of Rada before that sinful altar. That whole somber Tuesday the image follows you around as you tend to your chores in the shop. You try to get rid of the scene, but no matter how hard you try, it sticks to your screen.

That is why you haven't noticed that it's already eleven and you haven't even set up the curlers and brushes yet. You're so impressionable, Marina. That little snotnose has unsettled your sacred routine. You wipe the formica counters with a cloth and with a moist paper towel you begin to clean the mirror when suddenly you see Milagros' face. Are you dreaming? No, it's her, all right, she's standing there by the door, watching you, staring at you without blinking. She's weighed down by the suitcase she's got in her left hand. Without turning around you watch her in the mirror . . . yes, it's her. She looks a little different because of those tight maroon pants she's wearing. "What do you want, Milagros?" you almost murmur, unable to look at her straight on, watching her face in the mirror. She takes a step forward and brandishes a twenty. In a soft but firm voice she says:

"Make me up in shocking red, Marina, and cut my hair any way you like."

You feel a slight trembling in your legs, but even so you can't take your eyes from the mirror as you watch Milagros become larger and larger. She's growing before your very eyes, assuming colossal proportions in the mirror. She begins to walk towards you, yes, towards you in search of an answer, in search of the answer she needs and that you will have to give her. You can't put her off now, Marina, look at her, look at yourself, what will you say?

PILAR,
YOUR
CURLS

Maybe she should consider wearing glasses. She felt slightly dizzy as she watched the words swim across the page, and she was able to straighten them out only if she concentrated. But it really didn't require that much concentration because the words before her exercised a strange fascination. Sometimes her hypnotic trance reached the point where she forgot about everything but that rapid succession of related meanings.

The incessant chatter in the background was a counterpoint to her thoughts, weaving in and out intermittently against the sound of warm air around her head. The other sounds around her were the constant hum of three hairdryers and the screeching of the city buses in the distance.

She didn't let any of this noise bother her because she was able to turn it into a make-believe curtain that became part of the scenery. It was just like wearing false eyelashes: they feel a little heavy the first couple of days, but then you get used to them.

The only thing that got on her nerves was having to read while sitting in such a conventional position. She preferred to lie curled up on a couch or stretched out in an exotic feline pose that many of her friends liked to criticize, but who cares, she liked it. She couldn't even file her nails while sitting under the dryer—and, let's face it, they were starting to look like a washerwoman's. She turned the pages slowly, savoring each line. Why did they insist on making these paperbacks so ridiculously small—ten inches by six—when so many readers had requested better bindings and larger print?

This time she had rushed in late and, what with the line of customers and all, she had grabbed one that had a somewhat uninspired title: *You Shall Return.* She'd picked it out from a stack of magazines and paperbacks because she liked the picture on the cover—was it a picture or a drawing?—it made her think of that picture of her when she was only seventeen. She had dimples and hair that was pretty straight which she wore in a pageboy cut that won her the nickname "Suzanne Pleschette." Some of the nasty ones changed it to "Fleshette."

She glanced at the cover again while smoothing out her skirt—she had to remember to let down the hem one of these days. She opened the book and was pleased to see lots of dialogue. She liked the first few lines right away: "Walking into the darkened bedroom she noticed the rumpled bed . . . . Duke had been looking rather pale these days. . . . his hair was sprinkled with gray." Dramatic lines, these, with just the right touch of intimacy. "Sissy was overwhelmed by a storm of indescribable emotions."

Wear glasses? The idea intruded on her thoughts. Why not? It all depends on what kind of glasses you pick out. Those huge tinted ones . . . Maurice would take one look at her and . . . . She could imagine herself hiding her face and Maurice walking in with that slightly clumsy gait of his that reminded her a little of Marlon Brando.

"You're looking lovely tonight, my dear. You have the air of a French intellectual fresh from her morning bath. Those black pajama pants with that crimson sash are stunning."

But wait . . . no. Maybe the glasses would make her look . . . old? Even if he didn't utter a word, she would know. Besides, neither Kate nor Betty, not even Sylvie wore glasses: they all had large brown dreamy eyes. Dreamy eyes? What are dreamy eyes? Probably a little humid-looking with just a hint of sadness. As if they were contemplating horizons . . . distant horizons?

She turned to her page and read about Sissy. "She was thin almost to a fault, with violet eyes." But even Elizabeth Taylor's were, what? Blue? No, *Cosmopolitan* said they were violet. That was in the article about that huge rock Richard Burton gave her "to match the lovely violet of her eyes." Violet eyes with glasses on, she whispered. An odd combination, perhaps, but one that Maurice would probably like. He also preferred older women. Remember, Maurice, the time you scolded me at that dance for being jealous without any reason? I was twenty-four and feeling old, especially since I was surrounded by all those young girls with their silly innocent faces. You put your arm around me and reassured me that you wouldn't trade me for a hundred young girls, not then, not ever—not ever, you said! And then you kissed me, you kissed me deeply.

She felt a weakness in her knees and crossed her legs, carefully covering her thighs. Whenever she let herself get into one of her sensuous reveries the same thing happened. She went from one mirror image to another and another and round and round till she was almost dizzy.

This time she avoided losing herself totally in that labyrinth and returned to her reading, slightly annoyed at having lost her place. But she knew the same thing had happened to her before. She probably should buy herself a bookmark, maybe one in mother-of-pearl with her initials engraved "P.A."

" . . . searing violet eyes." Yes, that's where she'd been.

How did Sissy Biter meet Duke LeMoin? In Cocke County. In that small town—a burg really—on a day like any other. Who introduced them? It was all so vague. No one would have guessed how it was all to turn out, not even her. For Sissy it was all so routine and yet so suggestive . . . he had overpowered her . . . handsome, distant, sullen, he'd swept her off her feet. It was like floating on a still lake and suddenly having waves . . . .

It was just like with Maurice. You arrived at the party early and were just about to order a Manhattan from the overly solicitous waiter when, as luck would have it, your girlfriend came over with Maurice in tow, calling out to you, "Pilar, this is Maurice. You know, the friend I've been telling you about." You stretched out your hand nervously, saying, "Pleased to make your acquaintance."

Then it was just like in a dream. He asked you to dance and in that half-joking flirtatious way of his, he asked if you were having a good time. You looked up at him and, in a voice that surprised you with its brazenness, you said, "Are you?" He was already steering you towards a dark corner of the dance floor, moving gracefully to the slow melody of a . . . a foxtrot? You never could tell slow dances apart. It's just a matter of rocking gently to music, moving your body against his . . . . But you'll never forget the words to the song they were playing. You christened it "Our Magic Meeting Song." Remember? The song's words are etched in your memory. You have often thought since then that the author—was it the singer?—had an incredible sensitivity very similar to your own. You would repeat the words over and over to yourself— you've always had a good memory for song lyrics. "Your breasts like two young roes that feed amongst the lilies."

Then someone told you it was entitled "Chapter Twenty-Four" and you thought, "What a dull title for a song," as if it were just one more blade of grass, when in fact that song was full of spiritual, melancholy things. Sometimes song writers do that just to attract attention with their eccentricities. That's the way artists are. That's life. Just look at jet setters when they're about to get married. What scandalous behavior! Like that Mick or is it Mike? Jagger and his Bianca. *People* said her dress was cut down to her bellybutton and that she showed up at the St. Tropez chapel dressed that way. How could the priest put up with that? I'll never understand it in a million years. But she did look so chic in that picture they took of her. She had that big hat on, with her hair so straight and long, so natural . . . .

You know, the more natural you look the better, like this Sissy here with her black pants "and her black wool sweater, with black boots. Dressed that way she might have looked just the slightest bit masculine but instead, the contrast made her look extremely feminine. Besides, with that silky black hair of hers . . . ."

Maybe she'd wear black tonight for Maurice. It was such a classic color, so elegant. He would love her in black.

"How do I look, love? Is this little number becoming? It's from Francoise. You know, that new boutique in the mall. Maybe it's just a little too see-through, but I have a feeling you do like it. If not, say so and I'll return it."

That's Maurice, for you. Possessive to a fault, demanding in his taste and final in his decisions.

She just loved his firm "No!" You couldn't change his mind when he uttered one of those. Sometimes she'd try to find a little gap that she could work her way into, gnawing away at it like a tiny ant, finding a way to change his mind ever so slightly. But that "No!" of his was made of steel. She had to admit, though, that she got a kick out of reliving those scenes when he would utter his final pronouncement on an issue. She could feel her legs weaken as she remembered the last time . . . .

Sissy Biter didn't seem to be such a sharp heroine after all. In Chapter X she still couldn't seem to understand Duke

LeMoin's complex personality: a tender man who hides his true feelings under a cover of harshness.

"'Do you find me a bit rough, Sissy?'

'Yes,' she sighed.

He wrapped his arms around her fervently as they rolled over each other onto the rug. He was breathing heavily, leaning hard onto her slender body . . . ."

She's really a silly one, that Sissy. She just doesn't know how to handle a man psychologically. If Maurice were to try to force himself on me that way . . . .

She went from the heat of the hairdryer to a garden path overhung with jasmine and roses. Maurice was there with her, leaning his body onto hers against a column . . . .

"Now, Maurice, honey, you promised you wouldn't until after the wedding. I'm saving myself for you. Sweet, sweet Maurice, I know you would never force yourself on . . . Maurice! Take it easy, honey, you've had too much to drink, Maureeeeeeeeee—"

She stretched her legs out to keep the woman under the dryer next to her from guessing what was on her mind. She closed her eyes in order to enjoy the full flavor of the growing dizziness that was enticing her to open her legs slightly.

Suddenly she heard the beauty parlor owner yelling, forcing her to open her eyes.

"Pilar, that was for you. Come out from under the dryer a sec. It was Juan on the phone and was he mad! He said you've taken too long so he's leaving the kids at the neighbor's because it's his night out with the boys. He said not to wait up."

Pilar pulled her head out from under the dryer and started taking off the curlers.

"It's the same old story, Millie. I'll come by tomorrow so you can comb me out. Hand me that brush."

"Take it easy, honey. Just take it one day at a time."

It was the tone in her voice that made Pilar feel even more depressed.

MAYRA
MONTERO

Many factors have contributed to my addiction to writing.

Had I been born in Reikiavick, I would have been a figure ice-skater, which is what I have always wanted to be. But since I was born in the Caribbean—more specifically, in Havana, where the only decent ice to be found is in freezers—I was given other options: gymnast, hairstylist or taxidermist.

Unfortunately, when I was twelve, I leaped over the patio and fractured my ankle; I'm allergic to hairspray and my inveterate weakness for animals keeps me from skinning them, even after they're dead.

All that was left for me was literature, so here I am.

THIRTEEN
AND A TURTLE

There was a scream which ended in Arturo's shaking her awake, making her sit up in bed, panting. After all, the nightmare did have its little variations. That morning, for example, she had been dreaming that she'd stepped out onto the balcony to shake the tobacco smell from her hair. It wasn't a cold breeze so she relaxed and leaned against the railing, letting it blow through her hair. So it really was an inexcusable fall, definitely the work of someone else's will.

"It's over now," he murmured, kissing her hair, which no longer smelled of cigarettes.

Teresa decided it wasn't worth going over the same old dream with him one more time at this hour. It would be better to go back to sleep and just be grateful it wasn't true. Tomorrow she would have to take it more seriously, not forget it—or try to—as she had done all those other times. She would have to take bolder measures: try to imagine the feeling of the fall, that indefinable tickle in the pit of her stomach, those windows whizzing by to meet the floors, and farther down, her impact against the pavement. Which side would hit first? She knew there would have to be a sharp pain somewhere, on her nose perhaps, or on her forehead, a vulnerable spot in such cases. That all-encompassing pain and then, after a few seconds, a definitive calm without sudden drops or stumblings of any kind. When she thought of it that way, it almost didn't seem as horrible.

Arturo kept his arms around her until her sobbing subsided.

"Go back to sleep," he whispered in her ear.

"Tomorrow I'll tell you all about it," she said, trying to keep the issue open. "Anyway, you know the story. It's the same one.

"I'll go to a psychiatrist. Anything," she added, with a desperation that came from somewhere in her sleep.

In fact, that vertigo had always been there, her constant companion, a kind of umbilical cord that was her connection to the ground. For there had always been those early mornings with their sudden drops, mornings when the only thing that could keep her head on the pillow was Arturo's hand.

He had known about it a year ago, almost as soon as they'd met. She had been able to confess it to him right away, and since then he had made her take monthly trips to construction sites where he would appeal to her from farther down the scaffolding, ignoring the scornful looks of the workmen.

"We'll *both* fall," she would call out to him.

But at best he would only get her to peer out from the second floor opening of an almost-finished elevator shaft. At those times she would hold onto her husband's hand with an iron grip, her fear turned into an idiotic rigidity that froze even her gaze. She would hear him as if from a great distance, without understanding his instructions, memorizing each detail of the landscape in order to keep her vertigo at bay. He had culled these unusual exercises from a specialist's manual and wisely imposed them on her. But, of course, none of this kept her from overhearing the story one day, a story he told with an almost finicky attention to detail:

"A turtle?!" she exclaimed.

"Yes. It was too much for the eaglet and he dropped her from a height of . . . well, from a height the likes of which you'll never get to enjoy in your lifetime. The poor thing, falling head first, thinking about God knows what. Endless space all around, the world about to burst open at the seams and that thick shell smashing into her brain. And she probably landed on her back; they just don't have any other way of looking silly."

Teresa smiled.

"See? You can't be completely safe anywhere." said Arturo.

"I know," she said, filing the anecdote away, a strange comfort on that sunny, vertigo-free day.

That had all happened before the heat wave hit the city, causing countless throbbing headaches.

To tell the truth, it was Arturo's idea. But, after all, there's nothing strange in wanting to get out of town during the summer like everyone else.

When they were shown to their room and she smelled the sea breeze, saw the coastline and the huge sliding glass doors, she was excited at the prospect of being at such an enormous height, a height she had never experienced before. For it was a fact that she and Arturo had turned those strange exercises, in which fear and the void were experienced alternately, into a kind of child which they nurtured. It was their only offspring, their link to each other, a hope they held onto, secure in the knowledge that someday she would be able to sustain it alone. Someday she would be able to walk out onto the balcony just as he did, breathing in the salt air, held up only by the concrete floor and the iron railing.

Thirteen stories . . . . No doubt about it: now it was simply a matter of pulling the drapes open and judging the challenge that stood behind those huge sliding doors. There was just an ocean, a couple of sailboats and an indifferent horizon. Then a lightly perfumed breeze suddenly reached Arturo, who quickly made his way to the balcony and put his arms around her.

Teresa took in every detail of that balcony. It was a small semicircle held in by arabesque ironwork and a metal railing that she was now leaning into.

"Careful, Tere," he said, encircling her in his muscular arms and legs, an anchor ready to respond to her slightest move.

"You're here now and I know I'm safe," she said, looking down at their intertwined arms and legs.

"You're doing fine," he would say after each session. "So let's go down for a drink, you need to calm down."

The drink was the finishing touch to Teresa's duel with height, a duel she seemed to be on the verge of winning at times. Her allies were her nightmares and that strong hand of his, always right there when she needed it, unwilling to be defeated. The same five fingers that would later tug at her, persuading her to join him in the pool or at the bar.

The first week she had gone down every day, forgetting her exhaustion as vacationers often do. But that morning she decided not to go down. She walked around the room for a while and thought she might write some letters or rearrange her clothes, but suddenly she was standing outdoors, sur-rounded by sunlight. She spotted the pool right away. That was probably where he was right now, diving into the deep end but quickly swimming to the shallow end to play with the toddlers, to hide his lack of skill. She made out a tiny dark head, just like her husband's, crawling around the surface of the pool. She remembered the camera and went in to get it.

Back outside, focusing the lens, making his hair come close then recede, getting his features more or less sharp, she took a position in her tight quarters—that narrow half moon—all the while never looking straight down because, even though she felt safe, how could she be sure? She heard the first click and thought of how they would both laugh about it later. "See if you can find yourself," she would tease. Then suddenly there was that gripping terror. It wouldn't wait for photos to be printed. It was above teasing of any kind. It was a fear that made her go pale and notice, for the first time, that wrought iron chair there. A harmless chair, sure enough, almost an extension of the railing, but why hadn't she noticed it before? It threatened to trip her now, make her stumble over her own feet, stumble out of that metallic half moon that had suddenly turned hateful. She imagined it catapulting her down to the sidewalk below.

She felt her pupils dilate, like those of an insect stupidly staring at the spider that is about to make a meal of its flesh. She crawled along the floor thinking that perhaps her exit was not very graceful, but it was all she could manage right now. Then she realized she couldn't move her arms, couldn't move at all. She began to whimper, grabbing onto the chair's legs, wishing she had a strong arm to cling to, an arm that was, at that very moment, probably creeping along the bottom of the pool to retrieve a lost toy.

She tried to gain time by memorizing each detail of the landscape, keeping her fear at bay. Now her head, jutting out between the railing, stopped its jerking motion. She didn't hazard a guess as to how much time had elapsed, for it was a matter of figuring in all those childhood Sunday dares from the second-floor balcony—a long story whose details had their own logic which she was only beginning to understand.

Slowly she began to get up, savoring each motion. She looked out over the zigzagging motion of concrete walkways down below. For a brief second, she imagined herself hurling the chair out there, then thought better of it because, for the first time ever, she felt herself gaining that peaceful mastery, a growing sense of solidity under her eyelids—and without any help at all from her husband.

Arturo was just coming in, barefoot and dripping wet, tripping over the furniture in his hurry. He stood before the glass doors, panting. There was the camera in her hand, the lens jutting out between the arabesques, saved by some miraculous balancing act of hers. Teresa's body was closer in, leaning slightly forward into the railing. She was busy moving her prey forward and back merely by turning the focusing ring.

"Tere," he whispered, trying to keep from startling her.

"I'm fine," she replied. "I tripped, or imagined I'd trip over that chair there. I didn't even see it, I swear, I came out here . . . . I thought I was about to die; but thanks to the shock, I'm cured. Look at me."

And she leaned over, looked down, and stretched out her neck like a waterfowl.

"Arturo, I think it's over for good," she said, dangerously lifting one foot.

He smiled, terrified, unable to understand her words as he alternately stared at her and at that ancestral void that excluded him, that had always excluded him except for her fear.

"Yes, I see," he said, growing impatient, gripping her ankle in fear. "But maybe you should come in now."

"But you can let go now, really. I tell you I'm cured!"

It took Arturo a couple of seconds to begin to understand, to weigh his wife's indifference, her illegitimate joy. A joy which had nothing whatever to do with him. It had to do with the wind, with that vertigo of hers which had disappeared just like that, without leaving a trace, without leaving anything at all for him to hang onto.

"I assure you, I'm fine," she repeated as she reached out to him for a hug. She got only a pained look that came from the other side of life, as she was propelled over the railing by a sudden movement. The movement of someone who was now watching her fall—like an enormous turtle—from a silent, brutal encounter on the thirteenth floor . . . .

VEINTITRES
Y UNA TORTUGA

Para José Luis González

El grito culminó con el zarandeo a que la sometió Arturo y que la alzó sobre el lecho, acezante. Porque la pesadilla tenía sus deliberadas variantes. Aquella madrugada, por ejemplo, ella soñó que salía a deshacerse del tufo a ceniza que llevaba en el pelo. El viento no era demasiado frío, por lo que lo dejaba hacer, reclinándose sobre el barandal, de manera que el resbalón fue imperdonable, francamente premeditado por una voluntad que no era la suya.

—Ya pasó— dijo él besándole el cabello que ya no olía a cigarrillo.

Teresa decidió que no valía la pena contarle lo mismo a esta hora. Era preferible dormirse nuevamente y alegrarse por lo bajito de que no fuera cierto. Había que tomarlo más en serio mañana, no intentar olvidarlo como otras veces y solucionarlo en el acto con recursos más audaces: imaginando, tal vez, la sensación de la caída, ese cosquilleo indefinible en la boca del estómago, las ventanas corriendo locamente al techo y más allá, el impacto contra el pavimento, ¿de qué lado? . . . Sería cuestión de un dolor agudo en alguna parte; en la nariz, por ejemplo, o en la frente, tan vulnerable en estos casos. Un dolor totalitario y pocos segundos después, esa calma absoluta, sin resbalones de ninguna clase. Mirado de ese modo, casi no le parecía horrible.

Arturo continuó abrazándola hasta que la escuchó sollozar en seco.

—Duérmete— le acarició al oido.

—Mañana te lo cuento— dijo ella tratando de no cerrar el capítulo—, pero es igual, ya lo sabes.

—Iré a un siquiatra, haré cualquier cosa— añadió con un dejo de desesperación onírica.

Y es que en realidad, el vértigo siempre estuvo allí, como un viejo y sólido cordón umbilical entre su memoria y el suelo. Imprescindible en los deslizamientos vertiginosos de la madrugada, cuando sólo la mano de Arturo era capaz de retenerla sobre la almohada.

El lo había sabido un año antes, apenas la conoció. Ella pudo confesárselo sin timidez y desde entonces Arturo la arrastraba mensualmente a las obras y ante la mirada burlona de los obreros, trataba de convencerla desde cualquier andamio.

—Nos caeremos los dos— le gritaba ella.

Y él sólo conseguía, cuando más, asomarla desde el segundo piso, por el raquítico agujero de un ascensor en cierne. En esos pocos minutos, aferrada a la mano de su marido, transformaba cómodamente toda su lucidez y su miedo en una especie de rigidez idiota que le paralizaba la mirada. Así lo escuchaba a distancia, sin entender muy bien sus indicaciones, pero tratando de memorizar el paisaje, distraer el mareo en alguna forma, esos extraños ejercicios que él le había impuesto, sabiamente extraidos de algún manual especializado. Claro que nada de eso evitó que una de aquellas tardes se enterara de la historia, narrada con una taimada minuciosidad:

—¿¡Una tortuga?!—exclamó ella.

—Eso. Era demasiado para el aguilucho que la dejó caer desde una altura. . . . Bueno, de las que tú no saborearás en tu vida. El pobre animalito bajando, ¿te lo imaginas? . . . La cabeza de Zenón abajo, pensando sabrá dios qué cosas. Tanto espacio por todas partes, el mundo por poblarse, como quien dice, y el caparazón romper justamente en su cráneo. La pobre caería patas arriba. No saben hacer el ridículo de otra forma . . .

Teresa sonrió.

—Ya ves que en cualquier sitio se corre peligro— dijo Arturo.

—Lo sé— admitió ella, acatando la anécdota como un consuelo brillante en aquel mediodía sin vértigo.

Pero eso había sucedido antes de que el calor se apoderara de la ciudad, tomando posesión de cada casa, de las sienes de la gente.

A decir verdad, la idea fue de Arturo. Sin embargo, nada había de extraordinario en el hecho de querer salir como todo el mundo, dejar la ciudad por unos días, como mandaba la estación.

No fue hasta que les asignaron la habitación que ella se percató de la costa, del aire cargado de salitre que se aspiraba por todas partes, excitada ante la posibilidad de una altura desmedida, totalmente nueva. Ya habían hecho de aquellas prácticas de miedo y vacío una criatura que alimentaban tomados de la mano, esperando el día en que ella lo soportara sola, con tanta entereza como él, abriéndose paso hacia el balcón, cualquier mañana y respirando afuera sin otro contacto que el concreto o el hierro trabajado bajo las manos.

Veintitrés pisos. . . . No cabía duda: ahora era cosa de apartar el cortinaje y valorar la aventura aún detrás de las enormes puertas de cristal. De pronto fue el mar, un par de botes, un horizonte que no importaba. Súbitamente el aire, un ventarrón vivificante que había llegado perfumado y débil donde Arturo, quien ya en la terraza lograba asegurarla por los brazos.

Teresa detalló el balcón: angosto, semicircular, detenido por un enrejado fino que ahora presionaba su estómago.

—Cuidado, Tere . . . — dijo él alertando todos sus músculos con un SOS multitudinario de brazos y piernas que dependían del menor movimiento de la mujer.

—No es nada— dijo ella señalando las manos entrelazadas—. Estás aquí . . .

—Sigues muy bien— solía decir él después de cada sesión—. Ahora vamos abajo, necesitas sedarte.

Era el epílogo de una suerte de duelo con la altura en el que Teresa llevaba la mejor parte, respaldada por todos sus sueños y la tenacidad de una mano poderosa que no se daba por vencida. Cinco dedos que luego, relajados y felices, tiraban de ella hacia el bar o la piscina.

Sólo que esa mañana decidió no bajar. La primera semana se había marchado, dejando atrás un poco más de calor y esa increíble habilidad que desarrollan los vacacionistas para engañar al cansancio.

Caminó un rato por la habitación, incluso pensó escribir algunas cartas y ordenar la ropa, pero de pronto desembocó en la luz. No se detuvo porque enseguida divisó la piscina donde Arturo seguramente se sumergía, abalanzándose sobre la sección más honda, para adelantarse de inmediato hasta los ridículos cinco pies de profundidad donde disimulaba su poca destreza jugando con los niños. Atisbó una cabecita, semejante a la de su marido, moviéndose sin rumbo en el agua. Entonces se le ocurrió lo de la cámara y en un momento regresó con ella.

Abusó del lente, llevando y trayendo el cabello, el rostro más or menos nítido. Tomaba posición desde su reducido campo, esa medialuna angostita que conformaba el balcón, evitando mirar verticalmente abajo, porque estaba casi segura pero, ¿quién le aseguraba? . . . Esa alternativa coincidió con el primer clic, aquella primera toma que luego resultaría tan divertida. Adivínate, le diría a Arturo, a que no te encuentras.

Y súbitamente, un temor que no esperaba revelados, que dominaba todas las bromas; un miedo inmediato haciéndola palidecer y tomar conciencia de esa silla, ahí adelante. Una sillita casi inofensiva, como una prolongación del trabajado acero de la baranda; menuda y negra (cómo no haberla visto antes), pero que implicaba un salto, un ligero cruzar de piernas que no había entrado en sus cálculos, no ahora ni en ese balconcito lunático, así de pronto, odioso.

Las pupilas comenzaron a dilatársele, embobadas por ese arrobamiento del insecto frente a la drosera que acabará por devorarlo. Se deslizó sobre el suelo y pensó que esa salida a rastras no era la más digna, pero probablemente la única que podía intentar. Entonces supo que era casi imposible levantar la cabeza, mover los brazos, impulsarse de alguna manera. Comenzó a gemir, asiéndose más tarde, ya entre gritos frenéticos, de las patas de la silla, añorando una mano que en esos momentos rastreaba el fondo de la piscina, buscando alguna cosa que los niños habían dejado caer.

Trató de retener el paisaje, memorizarlo, entretener al temor y ganar tiempo. El rostro dejó de convulsionarse entre los barrotes. Había transcurrido un tiempo que ni siquiera intentó definir, porque se trataba de una vieja cuenta, que databa de domingos infantiles trepando aleros que entrañaban las más eficaces amenazas.

Se levantó cuidadosamente, con incorporaciones dulces, atalayando con una repentina serenidad los minúsculos altibajos del concreto allá abajo, desechando para siempre la tonta posibilidad de lanzar la silla, reconquistando sola, por primera vez y sin la ayuda de su marido, esa paz estática y dura bajo las pestañas.

Arturo entraba en ese momento, descalzo y empapado, atropellando exactamente todo lo que no estaba en su camino, porque una torpeza atroz los indujo a correr por los demás. Sofocado, se detuvo junto a la puerta de cristal, avistó la cámara, a salvo por un milagro de equilibrio. Un poco más a la mano, Teresa, blandamente atareada sobre la baranda, graduando la mirada en un rapiñoso enfocar y desenfocar de sus presas.

—Tere . . . — le dijo suavemente, evitando alterarla.

—Estoy bien— repuso ella—. Tropecé, o me imaginé que tropezaba con esa silla. No la vi, te juro, salí tan contenta. . . . Creí morir, pero gracias al susto. . . . ¡Mírame!

Y se inclinó un poco, mirando hacia abajo, alargando el cuello, presa de una encantadora seducción de flautas.

—Creo que se acabó, Arturo, para siempre—dijo levantando peligrosamente una pierna.

El sonrió aterrado, pero incapaz de comprenderla ahora que la veía claramente, alternando con aquel vacío ancestral que lo excluía.

—Ya veo . . . — dijo impacientándose, muerto de miedo, aferrándose al tobillo desnudo—. Pero es mejor que entres.

—Puedes soltarme— dijo ella, en confianza . . . — ¡Estoy curada!

Arturo tardó segundos en comprender, en evaluar la decidida indiferencia de su mujer, esa felicidad de una manufactura ilícita que no tenía que ver con él, sino con el viento y ese vértigo que desaparecía así porque sí, sin dejarle un margen a su orgullo.

—Te aseguro que estoy bien— repitié ella cuando iba a abrazarlo y sólo obtuvo una mirada dolida, ya del otro lado de la vida, precipitada por un certero movimiento del que la miraba bajar, como una enorme tortuga realizada en el brutal encuentro, tan silencioso e irreal a la altura del piso veintitrés . . .

LAST NIGHT
AT DAWN

This morning it all seemed less real to her somehow, unexpectedly dreamlike, like something that slipped away from the recent past. Last night's events began to seem merely imagined.

Perhaps the idea will take root that they both actually did go to bed as always, each one at the usual time, that there really was no long visit with those women, no incessant chattering until midnight. Perhaps too, the notion that earlier there had not been an hour-long nap in the afternoon, the heaviness of two days of rain plus that hangover from drinking Chateau Latour '71 at lunch, a vintage which had always been superb but which turned out to be unexpectedly acidic that Sunday afternoon.

But maybe, after all, things will be faced squarely and courageously and it will be admitted that those events did, in fact, take place, that last night life had taken a final, unexpected turn. There is, after all, the evidence of her fractured ankle, an injury that turned into a throbbing barometer when the slow, steady rain became a downpour around one a.m.

That tiny bone creaked like a fried chicken wing inside a cast made unusually heavy by the humidity. She knew the incessant rain would make the ceiling break out into dozens of sand-filled pustules that would later discharge their fine powder slowly onto the floor on the first sunny day of the season.

The termites arrived around ten, when the guests were having their coffee. It was an out-and-out invasion, led by a scout who had traveled through thickets of hideous cobwebs that now collected into a kind of helmet that he couldn't shake off even with the most vigorous tossing of his head. The vanguard's prank claimed five or six victims who became agitated for a few seconds. Then the rest of the troops emerged, fluttering around in spirals, stupidly gleeful around the five lights that had been placed in different corners of the room with an almost termite-like stupidity, given the fact that those lit-up corners were ones nobody used for reading; they were corners everyone would have preferred to leave dark.

One of the guests, a woman, suggested they place a container of water on the floor. She was sure the termites would dive right in, with a precision and an innocence free of either narcissistic or kamikazean impulses. But they all soon agreed that it was too late since the termites had spread out all over the ceiling, and it was probably not possible to fool every single one.

Later in the evening, the women left, dusting off fragments of tiny wings from their clothes, asserting that, yes, it was definitely the season for them, and describing in great detail the termites' repulsive yearly transformation. It was a somewhat boring if symbolic metamorphosis after which, ragged and hungry and moving about in the shape of worms, they would begin to devour the rattan furniture and whatever other delicacies they found in their paths.

So the ladies left around midnight when the rain let up briefly. Around one she decided to read for a while on the terrace because she wasn't sleepy and her husband, asleep in the bedroom, resented the light of her reading lamp and her steady turning of pages.

"It sounds exactly like giraffes chewing," he would grunt, taking refuge under a pile of pillows and shaking the bed in annoyance.

So she shut the bedroom door. The rain had let up a bit; it was finally almost stopping as she hobbled over to the plant-filled terrace on her crutches and lowered herself into one of the creaky bamboo chairs.

She was about to turn on the light when she heard the dull, metallic sound of someone entering her next door neighbor's van. It took a few seconds before she registered that it was not the man next door there, and that the blurred outline of a head moving inside that cheery van had much about it that was illicit. The shadowy silhouette was stretching up, scrutinizing the now brightly lit terrace and, with a periscopic insistence, was trying to position itself so as to have a clear view of that woman looking down at him. His look was an attempt to gauge those painful steps in their hobbled choreography. There was something about that laborious syncopation of rubber-tipped crutches on the floor that was tempting, something that provoked the imagination to dream up some vague misdeed capable of monopolizing Tuesday's headlines.

If she had not been sure the downstairs door was locked, it all would have ended right there because she would have rushed to awaken her sleeping husband so that he would go down and check. Of course, that in itself was no guarantee, as the man could still have returned tomorrow, the next day, or even next week at some careless moment, and by then they would have completely forgotten about how they'd come between him and this godforsaken rain, between him and his booty. And how would they even begin to guess, with their bright terrace lights and their racket—which the husband would make in order to give the man time to get away—that he would note each and every feature, each gesture and move, so as to record it later for the use of one of his many friends committed to carrying out those inexorable tropical vendettas.

But of course the downstairs door was locked and it was just a matter of sitting down to read that article about the feeding habits of boa constrictors. Right then there was another wave of termites. They filled the terrace, dropping tiny wings like muddy shoes, madly seeking hidden dwellings, spaces that would presumably be dry and comfortable enough for them to reside in now that they had discarded their angelical garb. She herself squashed two that tried to enter her cast by making for the pale, tender flesh of her grape-like toes. Her toes insisted on moving around with that claustrophobic tendency feet have to remove themselves from the rest of the body. They were turning hot and cold by turns now with a stubborn insistence that was beyond any anatomical principle she knew of.

So, knowing he was there in the van, she sat motionless, holding in her breath, turning nonsensical thoughts around in her head. She was briefly distracted by the shower of tiny wings that was coming down steadily, including, at one point, a whole termite body which landed on the article about boa diets. She smacked it to a pap with her left hand. For one long moment, she hobbled around on one foot and listened to the other foot crackle like a muffled saltine while she mouthed obscenities under her breath. The bamboo chair fell to the floor with a crash. Throughout, she was aware of the man's head there behind the windshield, immersed in his patient vigil, waiting for her to go on in to bed. After all, it was already two a.m. and she couldn't possibly plan to read all night.

That was when her fury sprang up, for suddenly she felt the full weight of her loneliness, a cold presence, complete and unforgiving, a solitude that, like the termites, had dropped its wings and was now dislodged from its moorings. Like the termites, too, it was fully mature, had come to a head and was crawling around like a reptile on the walls, between the furniture, through the cast on her leg and even over her own skin. She was bending over to pick up the article about boa constrictors that had dropped to the floor in the commotion when she began to grapple with that dissatisfaction. She paused to struggle with it and, perhaps, who knows? even to feed it from within because, after all, it was the man downstairs who was the intruder; it was he who was imposing an unexpected presence on her, a presence she had not counted on that night. That figure was demanding more than she was capable of contending with right now, not to mention the fact that he was in the act of stealing her next door neighbor's van.

She wanted to yell out that he was free to go ahead and take it. That, in any case, it would probably be better if he would just take off in that neatly parked van. That he was free to screech out of there and make as much noise as he wanted to, for she would be the only witness. That there was no need for him to wait because she really couldn't care less. But he refused to allow her the pleasure of her generosity, even though he could tell that her gaze did impose one condition: it would be just this once; next time she'd have to see.

He didn't budge. She leaned against the railing. After ten or twelve minutes her eyes filled with tears. His patient inertia became an unbearable weight, exhausted her—she who had all the advantages. She had only to call out and her husband would put an end to that human fishbowl drama. Perhaps then, with sirens blaring and neighbors pouring out, even the termites would make their exit.

But she knew she was incapable of calling anyone. She sensed that the man down there, by merely discerning her figure through glass and railing, by merely looking up through the windshield as if into a dream, had suddenly gained the upper hand.

Then she leaned harder into the bars as if by doing so she would finally manage to see into the man's eyes and exorcise the terror. It was a fear he probably felt too, as he watched her sobbing, moaning and then openly crying into the darkened street. His fear turned into a frenzied attempt to start the van; to make his getaway from that weeping, that sudden gesture with which she dropped the crutches and ripped open her bathrobe.

He caught a glimpse of her breast, her tears, the shower of tiny wings that almost covered her face, as he tried once more to start the engine, determined to make it go this time. Three, four tries without looking up at the grotesque tableau on the terrace; on the fifth try he was successful and the engine started with a dull pop. He looked up at her. She was slumped against the railing. He gazed at her with an expression that tried to take in the enormity of their loss; his face and shoulders spoke volumes in a gesture that would never be repeated. He succumbed totally to looking at her and she, for her part, imagined his dark eyes that seemed dissolved in that barely visible face. Now that the van had finally been tamed, his eyes would probably light up. Yes, they would light up now, but she knew that they would be the eyes of an ally.

She stopped crying then and began to take in that look, a look she welcomed like the arrival of an old friend. She saw him lower his head in despair; it was a weariness she knew well and could discern in any gesture. Now it was as if they were both stealing the van, content or nearly content, making it lurch along and pick up speed at the corner, watching it turn the corner and silently, almost gently, disappear into the darkness.

CARMEN VALLE

Photo: H. Zurita

I started writing when I was young and didn't know that what I was doing was "writing." Much of that material was lost—I lent it out and friends don't return things—but, since I was writing all the time, I didn't waste any time thinking about such details. Of course, I still have many of those unpublished first writings. Once, I went back and read some of them and realized that I started writing because I read a lot. I enjoyed inventing other worlds with other inhabitants; I loved observing and appropriating details which I then used to remake those worlds to my own liking.

Words delight me; they irritate me; they incite and accost me; at times they pursue me. It is through them that I can approach much of what I don't understand; they allow me to pose certain questions. At the same time, I realize they have taken charge of me and on many occasions they say things and tell tales that even I cannot explain. Sometimes, even though I can, I do not explain. They should be able to defend themselves. I merely hunt.

DIARY
ENTRY #6

███████████████████

Maybe Renee's right. Maybe it's all a combination of fate and inertia. But just because I live this way, wrapped in filthy rags, doesn't mean I like it. I tried it differently, looked for a shelter that would take me in, even faked an illness once so I could get into the hospital. I made myself get used to the idea by telling myself that from now on I'd stop picking things up off the sidewalk and from trash cans, period. I started going to the park to simply sit in the sun. I would take my two shopping bags along, and I would resist any temptations I passed along the way. I even saw a perfectly good suitcase out on the curb and walked right by it. If I felt cold, I'd just pull out another sweater. For lunch I'd get a pretzel from the guy with the stand on forty-second and eighth, some soup at the church at night, then off to the subway station where the cops already know me. I'd sleep on my bags and that was that. Till today. This morning I saw a striped olive wool glove by that school. Beige stripes it had. I peeked at it out of the corner of my eye. I walked right on by. I got way past it. But it drew me back. It had soft flat fingers spread out there on the sidewalk, and it seemed to beckon. I turned around quickly before anyone else could notice it and pick it up, or before its owner realized she had dropped it and came back. I picked it up. Soft. Then I started fighting with myself, cursing and crying. I twisted it around in my hands and dabbed at my tears with it, not even hearing their remarks . . . look at that filth on her . . . this city's going to the dogs . . . you'd think we didn't pay taxes . . . I couldn't agree more. But I kept right on crying. I wanted to keep that woolen glove because what if they don't let me into the shelter or what if they let me in then I change my mind and run away? I can't stand those places with their schedules and their curfews and their once-a-week funerals, and I hate having them tell me what to do. That's why I never married. An apartment? Please, not that! I can't stand to have anyone hanging around me. Even Renee, with her hints all the time that I could move in with her. She does it out of friendship, I know, because she knows how I live, though she hasn't seen me in years. I know, I'll call her without telling her where I am. That way she won't be able to find me. What a shock for her to see me dressed this way . . . why am I talking about Renee . . . the glove . . . that crowd . . . the cop. I should give it a try, I have nothing to lose. I could live with her for a while. But what if I want to leave and she has me committed?

The bag lady glared at me with a look that said, "How dare you sit on the bench where I come to do my thinking?" She got up, walked a few paces and threw the glove at me. It landed on my lap. I didn't budge. I was paralyzed with fear. She spun around, grabbed the glove and was off. When I finally got up to leave, I could barely make out her tiny figure galloping off like a carousel horse with its saddle bags flapping at its sides.

DIARY
ENTRY #1

Now that the funeral is over, I want to be alone and write. I feel a little sad, but to be honest, not that sad. After all, my tie to Pedro was a combination of old habits and fear. There were times when I'd wish he would just die and never come back from his all-night parties. I would stand by the window at dawn and pray he would return, then I'd maniacally wish he would smash his car into a pole. Now he's dead and I am going to miss him. But I'll have plenty to do around the house and on the farm. I'll start off with the patio. First I'll get rid of those fighting-cock cages under the dining room window and replant the hydrangeas he made me pull out so he could keep an eye on the roosters from the house. I'll get someone to take them away tomorrow morning; I'll even give them away if I have to.

He sure was something . . . like when he would unexpectedly bring home lobster for lunch and cook it up for us in a vinaigrette. (I would have it with chablis while he drank beer; he never did develop a taste for wine.) I loved him . . . and I hated him. I'll never forget the first time I complained to him about staying out late after one of his cockfights: he hauled off and punched me so hard I was knocked unconscious for hours. When I came to, there he was, sobbing like a baby, rubbing alcohol on my forehead. A few weeks later, when he walked in at dawn and found me fuming, he put a gun to my head and told me I'd better shut up if I knew what was good for me. That's when I stopped complaining. There was no point in threatening to leave. I was pregnant and, anyway, he would find me no matter where I went. He would tell me that he loved me too much to ever let me go. Besides, he wasn't going to let any woman do that to him. I believed everything he told me and I feared him. I despised him, but I envied him, too, because I didn't have half the guts he did. After Augusto was born it got worse. He would tell me that if I ever left and took the baby, he'd put a bullet through both our heads. I believed him. He was capable of doing anything. Like the time he forbade me to go shopping without giving me any good reason and I grabbed my purse, climbed into the car and took off. He pulled out his gun and shot out all four tires, then he ran the car all over the farm till there were no tires, no inner tubes, no rims, just those sharpened axles that made the car look like a metallic pig turning on a spit.

I finally stopped loving him. But I always felt a certain pride about his generosity. He would do favors for any poor devil who needed them and he'd never ask for anything in return. He was even extravagant. For our anniversary he would take me to a jewelry store in San Juan, pull out his checkbook and pay for whatever struck my fancy, no matter how expensive it was. Then, too, whenever he would wear a tie and jacket, he was the handsomest man at the club balls, with his broad back, his well-groomed salt and pepper side-burns and mustache. Handsomer than even the younger men because, let's face it, he was no longer young, but then again, neither was I. This was a factor which kept me from leaving him as well. What could I do? I who had never practiced as a pharmacist because he didn't want me to work. I who had no friends of my own; all our friends were our friends. Plus how would I ever pay for Augusto's tuition, the house, the club dues and the maid? At forty I was just waiting for some grandchildren so I could relieve my boredom.

Now he's dead and I feel a little sad, but deep down inside I know that what they're saying is true.

"Now Flora can finally rest, poor thing. You know how he would treat her."

Now I'm free and things are going to be different around here. Tomorrow morning I'll start in on the garden just as I'd planned. But maybe I should wait and talk to Augusto first, he might not want to get rid of the fighting cocks right away . . . .

ANA
LYDIA
VEGA

Photo: Christina Tourdot

Ana Lydia Vega's latest book, *Pasión de historia . . . y otras historias de pasión,* takes the detective genre and gives it an irreverent feminist twist. A professor of French and Caribbean literature at the University of Puerto Rico, Vega is known for her ironic wit and her acerbic subversion of language. Her writing has won her numerous literary prizes, including the prestigious Casa de las Americas award for her collection of short stories, *Encancaranublado y otros cuentos de naufragio.* Vega was the co-author of the successful film, *La gran fiesta.* She is currently at work on an anthology of essays to be entitled *El tramo ancla.*

THREE
LOVE
AEROBICS

one

Una starts to nod off during the late news. She makes a supreme effort and stays awake to the end, then drops off to sleep.

The curlers dig into her skull and the alarm goes off near her ear. Una reaches over and presses down the button. Contract, relax, contract, relax, all to a slow count of six, then some deep breathing and an internal repetition of her all-purpose mantra, her tension reliever, stress exorciser and dissipator of painful thoughts all rolled into one. She relives her boss's latest insult, her recent battle with her kid's father over missed child support payments, the landlord's notice barring nighttime plant watering. Una remembers those five gray strands subverting the ebony of her hair, that steadily encroaching cellulitis, that throbbing in her left breast whenever she shows off by lifting a heavy weight. With all that information knocking, she knows she can kiss her beauty sleep goodbye. Rosy-fingered dawn is here with a vengeance now—despite her exhaustion. That little nap she took between first waking and before the alarm went off was devoid of even the questionable solace of dreaming.

Una unravels the cocoon of sheets around her. She can't find her slippers. A head cold threatens, but still, she lowers her feet down onto the icy floor, Grandma's warning about foot cramps ringing in her ears. All she gets is a gritty coating of soot on the soles of her feet. That's what you get for putting off mopping.

Una rinses out the coffee pot, throws away yesterday's grounds, turns on the stove and closes the refrigerator door left ajar by her son before he took off for the weekend with his dad. She pulls out the melted butter, sticks a couple of limp slices of bread into the toaster and puts the coffee pot on the only working burner. Off to the bathroom to rinse out her mouth, wipe off cold cream and follow it with a wipe of astringent. Una takes off her bathrobe—a garment laden with memories of a happy marriage—and tosses it into the hamper with the rest of the dirty clothes. She scurries into the kitchen in the raw as smoke from burnt toast fills the room. No time now to make more toast, but anyway, her midriff bulge doesn't need those extra hundred calories. She brushes her teeth and rinses her feet, saving her shower for later. She decides to break in her new shoes.

She hooks her bra, pulls on her pantygirdle. The low-cut blouse she's picked out gets caught in one of her curlers— and when she removes the responsible curler, she discovers her hair is still damp. Una starts to lose it and scrambles to find the blower, which is never where she remembers leaving it. Lo and behold there it is, but by now it's going to have to be the punk look whether she likes it or not. Dripping with sweat and starting to get into a real mood, she releases an expletive from the very depths of her soul. The line she always draws so carefully over her crow's feet is lopsided.

Her purple tube skirt is wrinkled. But Una pulls it on anyway, trusting her curves to iron things out. She grabs her purse and is about to leave when she remembers the most important detail. She sits on the stoop, pulls out a mirror and applies a thick coat of mauve lipstick to her pursed lips.

She wishes she hadn't given up the car in exchange for the furniture. She's got to take the bus. And it's quite a different story on Saturdays. The busdriver's taking his time about it. Folks on line are being loud. Una knows she's late, she's got very little time left, and if she doesn't make it in the next few minutes, she'll have wasted a whole week.

The bus finally pulls up, a glorious orange gourd on wheels. Una hangs onto the strap for dear life. Her perfume fills the air. Nasty looks abound.

The bell is not working. An irate rider won the last round. Una is tense with a fear of missing her stop. The bus moves along slowly as Una sways through the crowd trying to get to the door. Of course, what with worrying so much about a missed stop, she gets off too soon.

Una's heels smack the pavement. Some trick moving fast in a tube skirt. Even with all the traffic, the bus passes her. Street numbers whizz by. Finally Una slows down, trying to breathe in time to her steps.

Changing her steps to a deliberate and languorous pace, Una comes to the corner where it all gets played out. She fights the impulse to beat a hasty retreat. Her palms turn clammy. Her heart is thumping away. But Una, in a magnificent show of mental control, cruises by slowly, indifferent as a duchess, her eyes fixed on a point in the distant horizon.

Is it a slight vibration in the air? An exuded warmth or aroma? Or perhaps all three combined? Without even looking, Una knows He's there, standing by the bar just as he always is every Saturday at nine o'clock sharp today and forever more. Una readies herself to enter into the orbit of His gaze.

two

He had already described to Her the very graffiti that witnessed an historic blow job, executed with great mastery by lips shaped in the *Deep Throat* tradition. Spread-eagled over the toilet bowl like an African king according to Tarzan, holding the door shut with one foot while countless anxious bladders waited outside for the moment of their liberation, He had had himself the come of the century, its fevered intensity surpassed only by the anticipation of being able to tell about it later.

Then She followed up immediately with a lucid memory of the languid hand job She'd administered to her cousin one Monday afternoon as they sat in the front row of a darkened theater in Santurce watching the triple x-rated *Coitus Uninterrupted.*

He, of course, felt called upon to respond with a faithful and thorough re-creation of the tableau He'd made with his boss's wife and daughter in their family room while the drunken husband cheered on the iron-fisted Durán who was bent on victory.

Which was immediately followed by the somewhat picturesque vignette of her unwillingness to refuse her best friend's husband's rearguard advances in her kitchen while they celebrated the new year. Given the disproportionate size of said husband, She had been forced to reach up for some Crisco while using her free hand to keep her own husband's dinner from hitting the floor.

All of which elicited in Him the nostalgic memory of his initiation into the arts of professional buggery on a beach in San Juan—as He rode the sunburned back of a broad-shouldered hulk of a gringo to the gentle strings of an old-fashioned orchestra, luxury hotels looming in the background.

She wasted no time in recalling the somewhat vague memory of her sessions of experimental lesbianism which her understanding sister-in-law had graciously offered on the day of her uncontested divorce.

Then He remembered his German shepherd and She her tawny pony, He his plump papayas and She her shaved zucchini, He his telephonic breathing and She her Tantric yoga. Then there was a sudden silence in tribute to all that remained untold.

Then He fixes his gaze on Her. And smiles. And says, with a voice that tries to be distant but can't quite manage it:

"It's a good thing you and I never married each other."

three

Everybody's divorced or getting divorced. Except us. It's going on ten years now. A record of married stability. And it's not that we're against divorce, you understand. When things don't work out, it's better to cut your losses and be done with it.

It's just that . . . well, it's a little embarrassing to admit that we're, well . . . *happy*. Seriously. It's pretty unusual, I know, but we're perfectly compatible. We have the same likes and dislikes, the same pleasures and joys. You say we have no children. But we've never wanted any. We're too busy enjoying life.

Some people resent our attitude. "Still at it?" they ask, trying to believe we can't last. They place bets on how long it will be before we break up; they talk behind our backs.

We just laugh about it. But it's no joke. A person could start thinking he's not normal. Could it be we're insensitive or just simply dull? Are we lacking in imagination or depth? What if it turns out happiness is only for idiots? But our contentment resists even those complexes.

In order to avoid unnecessary conflicts we never go to parties. Anyway, we have no juicy gossip to share, no family tragedies. When we come across someone recently divorced, we wave to them from a distance and let them go by.

We thank our lucky stars and go on our easy way, safe in the knowledge that, come hell or high water, for richer or poorer we're happy as larks—all three of us.

ADJ, INC.

███████████████████████

"Hate oppression; fear the oppressed."

—*V.S. Naipaul*

On the second of December, 1990, the Corregidora General blew a fuse. The rage she had been trying so hard to contain finally exploded. Leaning down hard on the intercom button, she had her secretary cancel all appointments and come in right away to take a letter. She then dictated the following urgent missive:

Dear Senior Benefactress:

Your letter of 27th November has unsettled us. But it gives me great pleasure to remind you that in seven years of uninterrupted operation under my leadership, the Agency has established an enviable record: 5,999 cases satisfactorily resolved. Our carefully monitored dossiers and the effusive letters of appreciation we receive almost daily from our clients attest to the fact that we aim to please and succeed admirably in doing so.

Statistics don't lie: 3,995 husbands rehabilitated and 1,994 corrected or neutralized. The Censor's Board was forced to recommend Final Solution in only ten cases, a tiny percentage considering the overwhelming success of our rehabilitation drive.

This brings me to the difficult subject of this letter, dear Benefactress, the purpose of which is to rid you of any doubts regarding the competence of either ADJ, Inc. or myself, its humble director. Case #6000 has monopolized our professional activity for the last four months. Due to its complexity and unique character, we are now in the process of reorganizing our entire executive branch. In light of the surfacing of this case, which may well be the harbinger of a new social reality, we have considered setting up an Unresolved Questions bureau to deal with this and similar cases.

I trust this initiative will go some way toward restoring your confidence and that of the other members of the Social Benefactress' Club so that we may once again enjoy a climate of mutual trust. This will allow your members to continue to provide us with generous and anonymous financial support as they have done in the past during our brief but efficient existence.

As per your request, we enclose photocopies of documents related to case #6000. We sincerely appreciate the interest you have shown in the resolution of this most complex of cases, and we ask that you call on us for any additional information you might need in your deliberations.

Hoping to hear from you at your earliest, I send you sisterly best wishes from everyone on our staff.

Cordially,
Barbara Z.
Corregidora
ADJ, Inc.

APPENDIX A
CASE 6000
CLIENT'S SWORN AFFIDAVIT

I, Porcia M., duly sworn notary and complaint recorder of ADJ, Inc., hereinafter referred to as the Agency, declare that on August 1, 1990, there appeared before me a married woman, a housewife and resident of San Juan, Puerto Rico whom, in the interest of privacy, we shall hereafter refer to as the Client. Client testified to us under oath that:

Whereas she has no cause for complaint regarding her husband, whose behavior to date has been exemplary; and

Whereas she thinks the vast majority of the nation's wives would envy her exceptional marital position since she is the unhappy partner of what she insists on calling the Ideal Husband; and

Whereas said Ideal Husband, hereafter referred to as the Accused, shares housework, is a good provider, is considerate, responsible, courteous, affectionate and faithful, as well as an efficient executor of all physical husbandly duties, lacking any defect other than his absolute perfection in every respect; and

Whereas the Accused's said perfection is an assault to the Client's self-image as it thereby calls attention to her own imperfection; and

Whereas in the interest of her mental well-being the Client feels an urgent need to file for divorce;

said Client, lacking even the faintest cause to justify such action, turns to the Agency in the hope that it will provide requisite pretext so that official rupture of the matrimonial bond may be initiated without further delay and with the celerity merited by the circumstances.

Sworn before me on this 15th day of September, year of our Lord, 1990.

Porcia M.
Principal Notary

Complaint Registry
ADJ, Inc.

_____

APPENDIX B
ASSESSMENT AND TRAINING DIVISION REPORT
RE: OPERATION ASSAULT

A preliminary screening revealed that the Client had behaved in exemplary fashion during her six years of marriage. Our conclusion was obvious: systematic subversion of this behavior was necessary if the couple's stability was to be undermined.

Client therefore attended our Exasperation Techniques Workshops I and II. Our Division offers these workshops free of charge as a service to the community. Client passed with a grade of "A+" and subsequently launched into a four-week "Operation Assault" program custom-designed for her by our training experts.

There were four phases to the operation, each methodically designed to bring about a crisis in the domestic system. Outlined below are the Client's evaluative statements on the success of each phase:

DOMESTIC SABOTAGE

"I took the opportunity afforded by my husband's business trip to cease and desist from all household cleaning. I let dishes pile up in the sink. The dishwasher was used to store paper bags. The bathtub had more than twelve rings in it. Bedsheets were rank with sweat and Vicks Vaporub. I piled dirty clothes everywhere and disconnected the fridge, letting shrimp and meat defrost and decay. I spread leftovers over the kitchen counters. Roaches invaded the greasy oven . . . ."

PSYCHOLOGICAL TERRORISM

"Just as I expected, my husband returned and, before I could bat an eyelash, donned his plaid bermudas and pulled on a pair of rubber gloves. He put everything in order in a flash. But since forewarned is forearmed, I had already gotten into bed faking dizzy spells and other symptoms, complaining about phony aches and pains and refusing to see a doctor. The poor slob thought I was pregnant. The joy on his face was almost more than I could stomach. It gave me a special delight to show him my stained underwear the following week.

"The following was the most difficult part for me, meticulous as I am about personal hygiene. I stopped bathing, despite the heat and humidity. I gave up brushing my teeth even after eating pineapple. I let my legs and underarms grow Amazonic. I threw out all brushes and combs so I wouldn't be tempted to comb my mane. Since my skin and scalp are dry, it wasn't long before I was scaly as an iguana. I had never been so wonderfully frightful; it turned my own stomach; I don't know how he was able to put up with it."

PSYCHOLOGICAL OFFENSIVE

"My husband's understanding and tenderness almost drove me insane during this phase. The phony tics which had been recommended came naturally. My eyes began to twitch and I developed cold sores on my lip. What's worse, for that long month of Operation Assault I couldn't even count on the Agency's moral support, as we had decided to cut off all communication to avoid any suspicion on his part.

"By this time I found it relatively effortless to yell obscenities at him and subject him to all sorts of verbal abuse whenever he spoke a kind word to me. Whenever he tried to talk on any subject, I would loudly yawn and act annoyed. I would refuse to go out with him anywhere. And if he asked me why, I would let loose with all the verbal violence I could muster. Insults and curses were the order of the day . . . ."

SEXUAL STRIKE

"I've never much enjoyed the pleasures of the flesh, anyway. My favorite erogenous zone is definitely my brain. That's why the final phase was not as much of an effort as the others. I simply denied him any intimate contact, turning away from him as soon as my head hit the pillow. This strategy, which would have been misinterpreted by any other husband, was actually my safest approach: his highly developed sense of fairness kept him from taking rearguard action without my consent.

"No king-sized bed had ever seemed so small to me before. In my overwrought state I just couldn't stop listening to his regular breathing. His slightest movement sent me into a frenzy and kept me from sleeping. I swear I could hear his heart beating. After a month of this, he was looking youthful and healthy. I, on the other hand, was on the verge of a nervous breakdown."

THE DIVISION'S RECOMMENDATION

Immediate transfer of case #6000 to Dirty Tricks Division.

Medea H.
Head Trainer II
Assessment and Training Division
ADJ, Inc.

APPENDIX C
CASE 6000

DIRTY TRICKS DIVISION
RE: OPERATION NO HOLDS BARRED

TRANSCRIPTION OF TAPE DEPOSITED BY OLGA THE CHEETAH, *AGENTE PROVOCATEUSE.*

Corregidora's note: The Agency claims no responsibility for the linguistic looseness of agents of this division. Please be advised that what follows is a verbatim transcription of an audio tape.

I was having me a well-earned vacation on the southern coast after dealing with about ten Accuseds in a row, each one a bigger mother than the one before him, when Dirty Tricks sent for me. Since I always put business before pleasure if I can't manage to combine the two, I gathered my duds and made for the Assessment and Training office. The boss lady gave me twenty-four hours to pull a workplan together. That didn't make me lose no sleep since I can check out any dude and tell you what his case calls for in two hours flat. After reading the statements and laying in some good brain time on it like I do, I checked out the photographs of the Accused in question. Especially the full-body portrait, child. No two ways about it. No problem dealing with this one: nice graying sideburns and temples, cute face, firm body for someone his age. But definitely not my type.

My first thought was: "piece of cake." These tall, light-skinned types, kind of cute, you know, Clark Kent glasses, the whole bit—they're usually a cinch. Nine out of ten, it's a case of they've been stirring it up since they were fourteen and by the time they've been married a few years, they can't wait to let it all hang out. That's where I come in. The only thing that didn't fit in with this dude's image were the three large onyx rings on the fingers of his right hand. I say *the* fingers because the other two were missing. Vietnam vet, I figured. But since that detail wasn't in the records I'd been given, I filed it away for future reference.

One of the chicks in Corporal Sanctions followed him for me for a few days, so as to catch his moves, you know. The guy was a case. He went from home to work, from work, home; no stops on the way. No bar, no pool hall, no health club, no chick, no nothing. Straight. According to the file, he only traveled once a year and that was on bona fide business. Maybe he fooled around while he was in New York, but as far as the island goes, nothing. No two ways about it, if we were to catch him in the act it would have to be staged right here and that's that. I figured the best place for it was his office.

One of our informers worked in the Personnel office of his company and she gave me the break I needed. As head of the unit, she figured out how to get me into his office by firing their receptionist and putting me in her place. I blew quite a wad on fine threads and makeup, and Assessment made me take a crash course in an office protocol and mini-finishing school-type program. But by November first there was yours truly at her post behind the reception desk with a low-cut dress with the knit skirt slit up close to my belly button. Then I grabbed me one of those Bette Davis cigarette holders and was off and running. They don't call me the Cheetah for nothing.

About a week after I started, I swear on my mother each and every one of the dudes working there was after me to go out—even the janitor. But mostly they were after me to go *in,* you know. Everyone but the damned Accused. And it wasn't that he hadn't noticed me; it was impossible not to notice me. Besides, he had to go past my desk every morning after punching in. I would about split a lip smiling at him, batting my lashes and leaning forward to conquer. Then I'd say "Good morning" in a voice that would make even a eunuch get hard. No dice. Modesty aside, nature has been good to me. At work they all know there's nobody can beat me at getting, processing and dispensing with the male element. But this guy was something else. With his California smile and his TV anchorman's politeness, he was driving me nuts.

I wouldn't miss a chance to sashay by his office during coffee breaks and on my way to the bathroom. I tell you, I would swing that thing. None of the other guys could get any work done watching me take my rolling strolls. A broken pencil point, a few photocopies to be done, any little thing was an excuse to go by his office. Sometimes I'd wait as long as an hour just to ride down the crowded elevator with him, then I'd seize the time to establish some breast-to-back physical rapport. But none of it made a dent.

Then to top it all off, his secretary started giving me a hard time. She was one of those walking antiques who'd noticed the moves I'd put on her boss and decided she'd take matters into her own hands. Every morning she would greet me with the scowl that launched a thousand craters, and one fine day in the copying room she came right out with it: her boss was a decent family man and I'd better lay off, this that and the other, including a few uncalled for remarks about the morals of yours truly. I lost my temper and suggested to her the reason she was making such a screeching sound was that her engine probably needed a tune-up and I knew just the guy who could do it for her. She turned purple and started threatening me with she was going to slap me silly, to which I responded with "You and what army?" which calmed her down some given she was definitely squat and out of shape to boot. Good thing she didn't try anything because, even though the Agency's policy is never to hit broads no matter how bitchy they get, that particular item was just about hollering for the good whack in the head I was preparing for her . . . .

They'd given me a deadline at the Agency and this mess with his secretary was slowing me down, so I had to take the bull by the horns and make my move. I went straight to the Accused and, in my huskiest imitation of Lauren Bacall, told him I needed to see him urgently when he was through with work. I slowly licked my lips so there would be no mistake about my meaning. He said, no problem, to wait for him at five, that he'd be there as soon as he finished "verifying some figures . . . ."

I was still pacing around at quarter past six, waiting for that half-wit to finish putting x's and circles in his godforsaken columns. I was surprised at my own patience. But the best part was, his secretary kept hanging around trying to see what I was up to in the interest of protecting her beloved boss's good name. Finally he says to her, "That's fine, Ms. Thelma, you can go home now. Good night." I gave her my best smirk and a look that said, "Chalk one up for the Cheetah."

To make a long story short, I used up all my leg crossings, all my stoopings to conquer, all my oblique approaches. And you know that when it comes to that, I'm the best there is . . . . Zilch. I probably could have taken a little longer with it, but when he asked me in that polite tone of his "what it was I wanted to ask him," I lost it. I leaned hard into him and started fondling his privates, panting into his ear. I thought for sure he'd respond if only to show he'd been put together right at the factory, you know. But before I could get more deeply into the issue he pushed me away and skipped out carrying that silly attaché case of his. He had a shit-eating grin on his face that made me think what fun it would be to rip his glasses off his face and grind them into a fine dust. And I would have done it, too, if it hadn't been that I was still figuring I could get him to play ball.

Next day I was fired. That son of a bitch reported me for "sexual harassment." I've never come across a specimen like this one before. There's just no way to lay your hands on him!

As far as the Client is concerned, in my book she's either a moron or one of those types that gets off on being punished. Why don't they send this hot potato over to Corporal Sanctions? Let Chiqui the Fist handle him. She likes nothing better than to give a well-earned smack in the head to any jerk who deserves it.

———

APPENDIX D
CASE 6000
SEXUAL REHAB DIVISION
RE: OPERATION MOTEL

At her age and considering the social costs involved in such an action, the idea of going to a motel with a strange man was not exactly to the Client's liking. But the impasse which had been reached, combined with her desperation, made her accept the plan. With the little that remained in the budget for this case we contracted the services of a well-known gigolo who was very popular in the resort areas. We hoped this would be the first and last time we would be forced to resort to the services of a member of the male gender in solving a case. We gave him money for clothes and rented him a car. We reserved a room in a motel near the beach in Caguas, a motel famous as a place for illicit trysts. Assessment decided on a place called "Swing Butt Low," their reasoning being that the lower the class of the establishment chosen, the bigger the insult would be.

On the 20th of November at three o'clock sharp, the contracted gigolo, one Sly Stick by name, drove up to the Client's house with the radio blaring. He proceeded to honk his horn and apply saliva to his eyebrows in the rearview mirror while he waited. Every effort was made to assure audience participation on the part of the neighbors. The Client had been instructed to make Sly wait a few moments in order to create some suspense. When she finally came out she was wearing a skin-tight crepe dress and spike heels. She walked over to the door Sly was holding open and the two of them tongue-kissed for a full 60 seconds.

They then screeched out of the neighborhood and made their way to the aforementioned motel. While participating in joint action at the motel, they were guarded by Chiqui the Fist in case any violence ensued.

The Agency had sent several anonymous notes to the Accused before the date of the meeting. On the day itself, Chiqui the Fist made the necessary phone call from a pay phone. She disguised her voice with her chewing gum as she does on these occasions. She very politely asked to speak to the Accused. She covered herself by faking a heavy Cuban accent and using an alias. When he got on the line, she hoarsely breathed into the phone (verbatim quote): "Listen, jerk, your wife's getting it on with some pimp in Caguas. She's screaming so loud you can hear her three miles down the road."

Chiqui asserts that just when she was about to give him the name and address of the motel, he hung up. This report was subsequently confirmed. Not only didn't the expected action take place as a result of the call, but the Client reports that, upon her return home, looking as disheveled as if she'd just spent the night performing sadomasochistic rituals with a band of banshees, she found her husband busy preparing a gourmet meal in celebration of their sixth wedding anniversary. The table was set with their best silver candelabra and their finest china and stemware. He didn't even ask her where she had been all afternoon as he was busy with the meal.

We have been forced to come to the conclusion that results have been inversely proportional to the effort expended on this case by our division. Our operations have been checkmated. I fear that case #6000 has set an inauspicious precedent in the history of ADJ, Inc.

Circe F.
Rehab Counselor IV
Sexual Rehab Division
ADJ, Inc.

The Senior Benefactress shuffled through the documents one last time before putting them into a manila envelope marked in red with the number 6000. A quick stroke of that salt and pepper mustache, a straightening of glasses, and then three onyx rings dropped into the top desk drawer. With a quick motion, the rubber gloves were pulled on tight.

A vaguely tender smile played on those lips while eight fingers efficiently typed on a piece of official letterhead the words:

BURN FILE.
SILENCE CLIENT.
ASSIGN #6000 TO NEXT CASE.

DIANA L. VÉLEZ

Photo: Alan Ross

Diana L. Vélez was born in San Sebastián, Puerto Rico. Her family emigrated to the United States when she was four years of age. She grew up in New York's Lower East Side, near Chinatown and Little Italy. She attended City College of New York and went on to Columbia University, where she took her M.A., M.Phil. and Ph.D. degrees in Spanish and Spanish American Literature. At present, she is an associate professor at the University of Iowa, where she teaches Spanish-English translation and Latin American literature. She lives in Iowa City with her husband and two cats.

▦spinsters | *aunt lute* ▣

Spinsters/Aunt Lute Book Company was founded in 1986 through the merger of two successful feminist publishing businesses, Aunt Lute Book Company, formerly of Iowa City (founded 1982) and Spinsters Ink of San Francisco (founded 1978). A consolidation in the best sense of the word, this merger has strengthened our ability to produce vital books for diverse women's communities in the years to come.

Our commitment is to publishing works that are beyond the scope of mainstream commercial publishers: books that don't just name crucial issues in women's lives, but go on to encourage change and growth, to make all of our lives more possible.

Though Spinsters/Aunt Lute is a growing, energetic company, there is little margin in publishing to meet overhead and production expenses. We survive only through the generosity of our readers. So, we want to thank those of you who have further supported Spinsters/Aunt Lute—with donations, with subscriber monies, or with low and high interest loans. It is that additional economic support that helps us bring out exciting new books.

Please write to us for information about our unique investment and contribution opportunities.

If you would like further information about the books, notecards and journals we produce, write for a free catalogue.

Spinsters/Aunt Lute
P. O. Box 410687
San Francisco, CA 94141